Professor Boris Bigalke, MD

The Enigma of the Mars Pyramid

Professor Boris Bigalke, MD, MBA (Oxford, UK), LL.M. works as an attending and head of the DGK CardioMRI Qualification Center at the German Heart Center of the Charité (DHZC), Campus Benjamin Franklin, Clinic for Cardiology, Angiology and Intensive Care Medicine. He also practices complementary medicine with Traditional Chinese Medicine (TCM), Traditional Tibetan Medicine (TTM) and yoga movement theory as a sideline. Professor Bigalke is a specialist in internal medicine and holds specializations and additional qualifications in cardiology, acupuncture, nutritional medicine DAEM/DGEM® and magnetic resonance imaging.

After studying medicine at the Free University of Berlin, he continued his scientific and clinical career at the Eberhard-Karls-University of Tübingen.

Further training led him to surgery at the LIJ Medical Center, Albert Einstein College of Medicine, New York, USA, to TCM at the WHO Collaborating Center, Beijing, China and to TTM at the Qusar Tibetan Healing Centre, Dharamsala, Himachal Pradesh, India.

During a long-term research stay, he also worked at King's College London, Division of College London, Division of Imaging Sciences and Biomedical Engineering London as an Assistant Professor/Honorary Lecturer.

He also completed a Master of Business Administration (MBA) Healthcare Management at Magna Carta College, Oxford, UK, and a Master of Laws (LL.M.) with a focus on medical law at the Dresden International University.

In 2021, Professor Bigalke applied to become an astronaut for the European Space Agency (ESA). Out of more than 22,500 qualified applicants, he was one of the top 100 candidates in Germany. Even though he did not become an astronaut, he has always been fascinated and inspired by space travel and our neighboring planet Mars.

Professor Bigalke has been elected as one of Germany's top physicians in FOCUS-Gesundheit 2021 in the category of cardiological sports medicine, and in 2023 and 2024 in the categories of hypertension and nutritional medicine.

Professor Boris Bigalke, MD

The Enigma of the Mars Pyramid:

Echoes of the Red Horizon

Disclaimer:

This book is a work of fiction. Names, characters, places and incidents either are products of the author's imagination or are used fictitiously. Any resemblance to actual events or locales or persons, living or dead, is purely coincidental. The content presented here is intended solely for entertainment. The book does not constitute a recommendation or promotion. Due to the fictional character, the content of the book does not claim to be complete, nor can the timeliness, accuracy and balance of the information provided be guaranteed. The author accepts no liability for any inconvenience or damage resulting from the use of the information presented here.
The author does not endorse or promote discrimination based on ethnic or national origin, age, gender, sexual orientation, religion, disability, military status, social-economic background or any other factor. This work aims to foster understanding, empathy, and inclusivity.
For better readability, gender-neutral wording has been omitted. All masculine spellings refer equally to all genders.

Address of Correspondence:
Professor Boris Bigalke, MD, MBA (Oxford, UK), LL.M.
Klinik für Kardiologie, DHZC – Charité Campus Benjamin Franklin
Hindenburgdamm 30, D-12203 Berlin, Germany

Bibliographic information of the German National Library:
The German National Library lists this
publication in the German National Bibliography;
Detailed bibliographic data is available on the Internet
can be accessed via http://dnb.dnb.de

The automated analysis of the work in order to obtain
information in particular on patterns, trends and correlations
correlations in accordance with §44b UrhG ("text and data mining")
is prohibited.

This book was translated by Professor Boris Bigalke, MD, from the original German edition titled:"Das Rätsel der Marspyramide: Echos vom roten Horizont"

Publisher: BoD • Books on Demand GmbH, In de Tarpen 42, 22848 Norderstedt
Print: Libri Plureos GmbH, Friedensallee 273, 22763 Hamburg

ISBN: 978-3-7597-5877-4

For everyone who wants to get inspired for Mars!

Contents

Introduction

Mars: The Red Planet with a Rich Historical and Cultural Legacy

Mars, the fourth planet from the Sun in our solar system, has captivated human imagination for millennia. Known as the "Red Planet" due to its distinctive reddish appearance, Mars has been a prominent feature in the night sky and has played a significant role in various cultures throughout history.

Connection to Mesopotamia

The Sumerians, who lived in Mesopotamia around 3500 BC, are one of the earliest known civilizations to carry out and record astronomical observations. The Sumerians observed the five planets known at the time (Mercury, Venus, Mars, Jupiter and Saturn) and gave them names. Mars was named "Nergal" after their god of war.

Connection to Ancient Egypt

In ancient Egypt, Mars was known as "Her Desher", meaning "The Red One", a direct reference to its color. The Egyptians meticulously tracked Mars's orbit, which contributed to their understanding of celestial mechanics. The name of the Egyptian capital Cairo (Arabic: ال قاهرة, pronounced "al-Qāhira") does have an interesting connection to the planet Mars. The name "al-Qāhira" means "The Conqueror" or "The Vanquisher", and it was given to the city when it was founded in 969 AD. Mars was rising in the sky at the time of the city's foundation, and the name was chosen to reflect the planet's perceived influence and to symbolize strength and victory.

Ares or Mars in Ancient Greece and Rome

The planet's reddish hue also influenced the ancient Greeks and Romans. The Greeks named it "Ares" after their god of war, symbolizing its blood-red color and the violence and destruction associated with warfare. Similarly, the Romans named it "Mars" after their own god of war, reflecting their cultural emphasis on martial prowess and conquest. This naming convention has persisted into modern times, and Mars continues to evoke themes of conflict and aggression in cultural references.

Beyond its mythological and cultural significance, Mars has been a focal point of scientific inquiry. Its similarities and differences with Earth make it a prime candidate for studying planetary formation, climate, and the potential for extraterrestrial life.

The Titius-Bode Law and the Missing Planet

In the 18th century, the Titius-Bode law, an empirical rule suggesting a pattern in the distances of planets from the Sun, predicted a planet should exist between Mars and Jupiter. When astronomers did not find a planet there but discovered the asteroid belt instead, it led to the hypothesis that a planet might have once existed but was destroyed or failed to form.

The asteroid belt contains numerous small bodies that orbit the Sun between Mars and Jupiter. The largest objects in the asteroid belt are Ceres, Vesta, Pallas, and Hygiea, with Ceres being classified as a dwarf planet. The combined mass of the asteroid belt is still much less than that of Earth's moon, which suggests that if a planet did exist there, it must have been relatively small.

Impact on Mars?

The idea that a destroyed planet in the asteroid belt might have had catastrophic effects on Mars is intriguing but largely speculative. There are several ways this could have theoretically happened:

Asteroid Impacts

If a planet in the asteroid belt was disrupted, its fragments could have collided with Mars, causing extensive cratering and potentially affecting its climate and geology. Mars' surface shows evidence of massive impacts, such as the Hellas and Argyre basins, which could be linked to such events.

Gravitational Perturbations

The destruction of a planet-sized body in the asteroid belt could have created gravitational disturbances. These perturbations might have altered the orbits of asteroids and comets, increasing the likelihood of impacts on Mars and other inner planets.

Atmospheric and Geological Effects

Repeated impacts from large asteroids could have contributed to the loss of Mars' atmosphere and the disruption of its magnetic field, both of which are critical for maintaining stable, habitable conditions.

Life and Living on Mars

One of the most compelling reasons for studying Mars is the search for water and life. Evidence of past liquid water, such as dried-up riverbeds and minerals that form in the presence of water, suggests that Mars once had conditions suitable for life. To date, missions aimed to discover whether microbial life ever existed on Mars.

The Drake Equation and the Fermi Paradox

The Drake Equation and the Fermi Paradox are central concepts in the discussion about the probability of extraterrestrial life and intelligent civilizations in the universe. The Drake Equation was developed to estimate the number of technologically advanced civilizations in our galaxy that might be capable of communicating with us. But many of these parameters are still highly uncertain and based on estimates.

In contrast, the Fermi Paradox refers to the apparent contradiction between the high probability of extraterrestrial civilizations (based on the Drake Equation and the vast size of the universe) and the lack of clear evidence for, or contact with, such civilizations.

Some possible explanations for the Fermi Paradox include:

Rare Earth Hypothesis: Complex life is extremely rare, and the conditions that led to life on Earth are unique.

The Great Filter: There is a stage or several stages in the development of life that are extremely unlikely, so few civilizations ever reach the point of sending interstellar signals.

Self-Destruction: Technological civilizations tend to destroy themselves (e.g., through wars, environmental destruction, or other catastrophes) before they can reach interstellar communication.

Isolation and Inaccessibility: Civilizations might deliberately isolate themselves or are technologically incapable of sending or receiving signals.

Technological Limitations: Our technology might not be advanced enough to detect or recognize signals from other civilizations.

Temporal Discrepancies: Civilizations might have existed or will exist, but are too far apart in time, so their signals haven't reached us yet or have already passed by.

Terraforming Mars: Transforming the Red Planet into a New Earth

Mars is the prime target for future human exploration due to its relative proximity and the potential for habitability. The primary objective of terraforming Mars is to create an environment where humans can survive and thrive. This involves increasing the planet's temperature, thickening its atmosphere, and introducing water and oxygen. One approach to warming Mars is to introduce greenhouse gases like carbon dioxide (CO_2), methane (CH_4), and fluorocarbons into the atmosphere. These gases would trap heat from the Sun, raising the planet's temperature. Another method involves placing large mirrors in orbit around Mars to reflect sunlight onto the surface, directly increasing the temperature. Heating the polar ice caps could release large quantities of water, forming lakes and possibly rivers, thereby creating a more Earth-like hydrological cycle.

The transformation of Mars into a second Earth represents not just a monumental scientific endeavor but also a profound statement of human ingenuity and aspiration.

Crew Members' Designation and Biography

In the not-so-distant future, when Earth's technological marvels reached their zenith, the United Mars Expedition set its sights on the crimson orb that had tantalized humanity for centuries.

Humanity stood on the precipice of its greatest adventure. Six astronauts, handpicked from different corners of the globe, embarked on a perilous journey that would redefine our existence. Their destination: Mars – the enigmatic red planet that had tantalized generations with its secrets. Their diverse backgrounds and conflicting personalities create a volatile mix.

The selection of the six astronauts for this unprecedented mission to Mars was no ordinary process. Each member of the team was meticulously chosen not just for their exceptional skills, but for their ability to adapt, innovate, and collaborate under extreme conditions. The mission required a unique blend of talents: scientific acumen, engineering prowess, physical endurance, and, above all, the mental fortitude to face the unknown.

The journey of these six astronauts began long before they set foot on Mars. It started with their rigorous training and the unyielding selection process that tested not only their abilities but their resolve and unity as a team. They were more than just colleagues; they were a family bound by a shared mission to explore the unknown and uncover the mysteries of Mars.

Their elite selection was not just a testament to their individual capabilities but to their potential as a cohesive unit. Each member brought something unique to the table, and together, they were greater than the sum of their parts. As they embarked on this groundbreaking mission, they carried with them the hopes and dreams of humanity, ready to face whatever challenges lay ahead with courage, innovation, and teamwork.

The beginning of their journey marked the dawn of a new era in space exploration, one that would test the limits of human endurance and ingenuity. This journey promised discoveries that would reshape our understanding of the universe. And it was this elite team of six astronauts who stood at the forefront of this monumental quest, ready to make history.

Let's delve into their journey!

Designation (Nationality):
Cmdr. John Harris (USA)

Position:
Mission Commander

Duties:
Overall mission success, safety of crew
and spacecraft

Biographic characteristics:
A seasoned air force pilot, John Harris is a no-nonsense leader.
He is a highly decorated military officer. He lost his wife in a traffic
accident, which still haunts him, but with the help of his military career, in which he had to experience many tragic blows, he has coped
well and even emerged stronger. His brawny build conceals a heart
that yearns for adventure beyond Earth's boundaries.

Designation (Nationality):
Dr. Emily Clarke (UK)

Position:
Pilot, First Officer

Duties:
Main control of spacecraft, scientific analysis and experiments in geology

Biographic characteristics:
Emily Clarke is an experienced pilot and the team's geologist. She has an amazing number of publications and research grants in the field of volcanology. She is a nerd and has gone through life very results and goal oriented. She is determined to uncover the secrets that lie beneath the surface of Mars, and perhaps beneath her personal surface as well, because she still hasn't found a life partner.

Designation (Nationality):
Dr. Ivan Petrov (Russia)

Position:
Physician, Second Officer, Copilot

Duties:
Crew's healthcare, supportive control of spacecraft

Biographic characteristics:
Ivan Petrov, a medical doctor and military pilot, possesses an athletic build and a brooding demeanor. He completed his doctorate in medicine in Germany. He is a dual medical specialist as a surgeon and cardiologist. He is very talented to play traditional folk music on the classical guitar with passion, which gives you an insight into his melancholy Russian soul. His past holds scars that even the vast Martian landscape can't erase.

Designation (Nationality):
Dr. Wei Li (China)

Position:
Mission Specialist

Duties:
Mission specific interpretation of pre-historic archeological relics

Biographic characteristics:
Wei Li, an engineer and linguist, defies stereotypes. Her tiny frame belies her fierce determination. She is a former Olympic champion in archery. She is fluent in eight modern languages and well-versed in classical "dead" languages such as Sumerian and ancient Egyptian. She deciphers ancient hieroglyphs with ease, unlocking the past. For physical balance, she practices Shaolin kungfu regularly.

Designation (Nationality):
Lt. Col. Sophie Dubois (France)

Position:
Flight Engineer, Copilot

Duties:
Technical maintenance, supportive control of spacecraft

Biographic characteristics:
Sophie Dubois is a helicopter pilot with an elite university diploma in engineering. She has a 2nd Dan black belt in Shotokan Karate and has mastered all 27 katas (prescribed shadow boxing moves). She is drawn to the mysteries of Mars like a moth to a flame.

Designation (Nationality):

Professor Klaus Müller (Germany),

Position:

Science Officer

Duties:

Scientific analysis and experiments of exobiology

Biographic characteristics:

Bald-headed and unassuming, Klaus Müller is a biologist and chemist. He is one of the pioneers to develop a novel approach to treat resistant pathogens and find ways to promote longevity research. Thanks to his humanist education, he is proficient in Latin and Ancient Greek, but also speaks five modern foreign languages (German, English, Spanish, Mandarin, Russian). Due to his knowledge of Mandarin, he automatically has special access to Wei Li and vice-versa. So does this have potential for more? His stoic exterior conceals a passion for understanding life - both earthly and extraterrestrial.

Spaceship Description

Let's delve into the details of the spacecraft, a sleek state-of-the art interplanetary shuttle. She is designated as The Ares Horizon in honor of the ancient Greek name of the god of war, the Roman pendant called Mars.

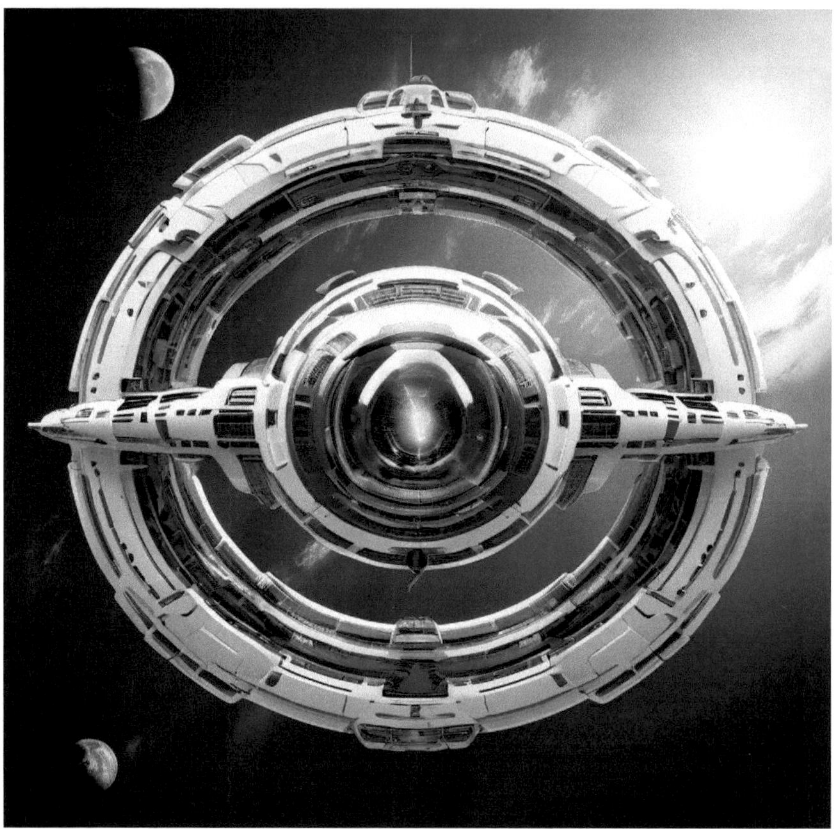

Spaceship Design

The Ares Horizon utilizes a cutting-edge propulsion system that combines magnetic principles and reaction wheels. Here's how it works:

Magnetic Propulsion:

- The spacecraft features a series of powerful electromagnets strategically placed along its hull. These magnets interact with Earth's magnetic field and the solar wind.

- By adjusting the polarity of these magnets, The Ares Horizon can maneuver without traditional propellants. It can attract or repel itself from nearby celestial bodies, alter its attitude, and even spin - all without expending fuel.

Ion Thrusters:

- For long-duration interplanetary travel, The Ares Horizon relies on ion thrusters.

- These engines accelerate ions (usually xenon) to high speeds, generating efficient thrust.

- Ion propulsion minimizes fuel consumption and extends mission endurance.

Reaction Wheels:

- The Ares is equipped with a set of precision-engineered reaction wheels. These gyroscopic devices allow the spacecraft to change its orientation by altering the angular momentum.

- When the crew needs to adjust their trajectory or stabilize the ship, the reaction wheels spin up or slow down, exerting torque on the spacecraft.

- This system eliminates the need for conventional thrusters, reducing mass and streamlining operations.

Artificial Gravity Ring

Encircling the central hub of The Ares Horizon is a massive rotating ring, aptly named the "Gravity Ring." Here's how it functions:

Centrifugal Force:

- The Gravity Ring spins at a constant rate, creating centrifugal force that simulates gravity for the crew inside.

- As the astronauts move outward from the hub, they experience increasing gravitational pull. At the outer edge of the ring, the force approximates Earth's gravity (1 g).

- This gradual transition mitigates the discomfort associated with rapid changes in gravity.

Living Quarters and Laboratories

- The Gravity Ring houses living quarters, laboratories, and recreational areas. Each section is oriented radially, allowing occupants to walk along the inner surface.

- The floor of the ring becomes the "downward" direction due to the centrifugal force, providing a familiar sense of gravity.

- Crew members exercise, eat, and sleep in this environment, maintaining physical health during long space missions.

Engineering Challenges

- Constructing the Gravity Ring requires advanced materials to withstand the immense stresses of rotation.

- Engineers carefully balanced the ring to prevent wobbling or vibrations.

- The inner core remains stationary, housing critical systems like the command center, propulsion controls, and life support.

Command Center and Bridge

Located in the stationary core, the command center houses critical systems:

Navigation:

Advanced star trackers, radar, and optical sensors guide The Ares Horizon through space.

Communication:

High-frequency transceivers maintain contact with Earth and other spacecraft.

Piloting:

A panoramic viewport allows the crew to observe celestial bodies during manual maneuvers.

Life Support and Sustainability

The Ares Horizon prioritizes crew well-being:

Oxygen Generation:

Algae-based bioreactors produce oxygen through photosynthesis.

Water Recycling:

Filtration systems purify wastewater, ensuring a sustainable supply.

Hydroponics:

The ship's garden provides fresh produce and psychological comfort.

Emergency Systems:

Escape Pods: Distributed around the hull, these small capsules allow rapid evacuation in case of critical failure.

Radiation Shields:

Deployable panels protect against solar flares and cosmic rays during interplanetary travel.

Conclusion

The Ares Horizon represents humanity's pinnacle of engineering — a sleek state-of-the-art vessel that bridges worlds, defies gravity, and carries the hopes of six astronauts who are ready to unravel the mysteries of Mars.

Chapter 1: Departure

The countdown echoed through the control room, each digit a drumbeat of anticipation. Commander John Harris, his uniform crisp, stood at the center of the command module. His eyes swept across the banks of monitors, each screen displaying vital data — the fusion engines' status, life support systems, and the trajectory that would carry them beyond Earth's grasp.

Beside him, Dr. Emily Clarke, the red-haired geologist, adjusted her spectacles. Her fingers traced the outline of Mars on the star chart. "We're really doing this," she murmured. "Leaving our home."

Dr. Ivan Petrov, the athletic Russian doctor and pilot, nodded. His jaw clenched, betraying the mix of excitement and nerves.
"Da," he said. "To the crimson world."

Dr. Wei Li, the tiny Chinese engineer and linguist, checked the communication array.
"Our families," she whispered. "They're watching."

Lt. Col. Sophie Dubois, the slim Frenchwoman with a penchant for adventure, twirled a lock of her blond hair.
"Adventure awaits," she declared. "And mysteries beyond imagination."

Professor Klaus Müller, the baldheaded German biologist and chemist, clutched his notebook.
"Our mission," he said, "is to unravel those mysteries."

The Launch

The gantry retracted, revealing The Ares Horizon. Its sleek hull gleamed under the harsh floodlights. The crew strapped themselves into their acceleration couches, their hearts pounding in sync with the countdown.

"Engines online," Ivan reported.

Commander Harris gripped the armrests. "Ignite, and… liftoff!"

The fusion engines roared to life, their blue flames swallowing the launchpad. Earth's gravity released its grip, and The Ares Horizon ascended - a silver arrow piercing the sky.

The astronauts felt the familiar pressure pushing them into their seats.
Emily's breath hitched.

Wei's knuckles turned white.

Sophie hummed a tune — a French ballad her grandmother used to sing.

Klaus scribbled notes, capturing the raw data of their ascent.

And Ivan?
He grinned, adrenaline surging through his veins.
"We're leaving," he said. "Leaving it all behind."

The View from Above

For several months the team has trained for this moment. At last, now they have made it!

As the atmosphere thinned, the blue orb of Earth shrank. The astronauts unstrapped, floating in microgravity.

Emily pressed her face against the viewport.
"Look," she whispered. "Our home."

Klaus joined her and said: "Yes, it is awesome, such a blue beauty! It is a pity that we still wage wars and make environmental pollution on such a jewel. Politicians should definitely get up here to reconsider their actions."

Emily enjoyed that she could share her impression with Klaus. She liked being in his company, had already felt that during the training missions on Earth. However, he remained level-headed and cool-headed with his emotional reactions — would that last?

Wei also enjoyed the breathtaking view, but also noticed the togetherness of Emily and Klaus. She couldn't rationally explain why this actually bothered her. She wiped the thought away and surrendered to the feeling of weightlessness.

Now she started to execute a somersault, her laughter echoing.
"We're weightless," she said. "Like cosmic dancers."

Sophie joined her, twirling.
"Next stop," she said, "Mars."

Chapter 2: The Long Haul

Despite advances in propulsion technology, the journey between Earth and Mars takes around 6 to 9 months. The time slot for the mission has been chosen according to the closest distance between Earth and Mars, known as opposition, which occurs roughly every 26 months. However, the distance at each opposition varies due to the elliptical nature of both planets' orbits. The closest oppositions, known as perihelic oppositions, occur when Mars is near its perihelion (the point in its orbit closest to the Sun) while Earth is near its aphelion (the point in its orbit farthest from the Sun). These perihelic oppositions happen approximately every 15 to 17 years. During long journeys, astronauts are exposed to cosmic radiation from two main sources:

Galactic cosmic radiation: this consists of high-energy particles coming from other parts of our galaxy, mainly protons and heavier ions. This radiation is continuously present and difficult to shield.

Solar particle events: These occur when the sun ejects large amounts of charged particles, mainly protons, into space. These events are difficult to predict and can produce particularly intense bursts of radiation.

The Cosmic Routine: Work

Scientific research:

Emily spent hours analyzing rock samples from Martian meteors brought back from Earth.

She meticulously cataloged the mineral composition and searched for clues to the geological history of Mars.

Klaus, the biologist, studied the effects of cosmic radiation on microorganisms. His petri dishes floated in the lab, revealing the resilience of life even in space.

Engineering Maintenance:

Wei tinkered with the spacecraft's systems. She recalibrated sensors, and ensured the fusion reactors ran smoothly. Her tiny frame squeezed into tight spaces, her toolkit floating alongside her.

Navigation and Course Corrections:

Commander Harris and Ivan collaborated on trajectory adjustments. They calculated gravitational slingshots around planets, optimizing fuel consumption. Their conversations were a blend of physics and intuition.

Rest and Recreation

Sleep Cycles:

The crew adhered to a strict sleep schedule. In the dimly lit crew quarters, they floated in their sleeping bags, tethered to the walls. Dreams of Earth—familiar faces, grassy fields—visited them in microgravity.

Virtual Reality:

Sophie escaped into virtual landscapes. She'd swim in digital oceans, climb pixelated mountains, and dance with avatars of loved ones. The line between reality and simulation blurred.

Reading and Films:

Ivan devoured classic Russian literature. Tolstoy's War and Peace floated beside him, its pages carefully turned.

Emily watched old Earth films — nostalgia for a world they'd left behind.

Camaraderie

Shared Meals:

The galley became their communal hub.

Wei prepared stir-fried noodles, Klaus brewed coffee, and Sophie told stories of French cafes. They laughed, swapped memories, and savored freeze-dried delicacies.

Personal Journals:

Each astronaut maintained a digital journal:

Commander Harris chronicled leadership challenges, whereas Emily wrote poetry about Martian sunsets, and Wei recorded her dreams — strange visions of alien landscapes.

Lecture Sessions:

On jeur-fixe dates, the crew members would give lectures to the others from their field of research and experience, except for Commander Harris. Although he has graduated from military academy with the rank of an officer, he is not a typical researcher or scientist. Therefore, he preferred to act as a host during these sessions.

Music:

Ivan's guitar echoed through the corridors and became the heart of their journey. He played melancholic tunes, folk songs, and improvised melodies. The crew gathered, floating, their eyes closed, lost in the music. Sometimes Sophie sang, her voice hauntingly beautiful. But Sophie also sang a cappella, for example old sea shanties or lilting tunes of French chansons.

Emily, with her geologist's precision, tapped out rhythms on the hull, turning the spacecraft into an impromptu drum set.

Wei, her fingers dancing over invisible keys, composed celestial tunes with the rhythmic beats of Chinese ballads.

And Klaus, during quiet nights, improvised harmonies with his lab equipment — a beaker as a bell, a pipette as a flute. Their music wove together the disparate threads of their cultures, creating a cosmic symphony that resonated across the light-years.
Sophie and Ivan harmonized perfectly as an ensemble.

Stargazing:

In the quiet moments between experiments and calculations, the crew gathered in the observation dome. Earth, a distant blue orb, shrank with each passing day. Mars, a reddish speck on the horizon, beckoned. Emily marveled at the constellations — the same stars that had guided sailors across oceans for centuries. She pointed out Orion, Ursa Major, and the Southern Cross. In contrast Ivan shared stories of the cosmos — tales passed down through generations. They traced imaginary lines between stars, connecting their own journey to the ancient myths.

Sports in Zero-G:

The microgravity of the spacecraft allowed for playful activities. Wei, privileged by her tiny figure, executed a perfect somersault, her laughter echoing through the metal corridors. Sometimes she met with Sophie to spar and practise Asian martial arts; Wei was trained in Shaolin kungfu, Sophie in Shotokan karate.

Klaus floated effortlessly, attempting bicycle kicks and mid-air somersaults. They played modified versions of soccer, basketball, and even synchronized swimming. Commander Harris refereed their matches, occasionally joining in for a zero-G slam dunk.

Sophie challenged everyone to a zero-G race, her competitive spirit undiminished by the vastness of space. Moreover, she was also able to inspire Ivan to take martial arts lessons together, she as a black belt karateka and he as a Systema specialist. The two of them seemed to be a good ensemble, and not just in the musical field. The vibes between them obviously worked out fine on different levels. They literally had close contact…

The Psychological Strain

The Ares Horizon hurtled through space, its crew finding solace in these simple pleasures.

However, as weeks turned into months, isolation gnawed at their minds. Earth was a distant memory, a pale blue dot. They missed rain, wind, and the smell of soil.

Ivan confided in Sophie, "I dream of birch trees."

She nodded, understanding the ache and added: "And I miss the sound of the waves from the sea, the chirping of birds and the smells of mother nature."

Sophie felt the need to hug Ivan. She made a cautious approach and he let her. The hug was good for both of them. Ivan said to Sophie, "You know that this releases the cuddle hormone oxytocin, so we'll both feel better again quickly. However, our embrace could be dangerous if dopamine and vasopressin are also released, then I can't guarantee anything." He winked at her and Sophie laughed briefly.

Sophie did indeed feel better quickly, but hid the fact that she was now experiencing feelings of familiarity and inner affection.
Was it perhaps even dopamine and vasopressin already?
Is this all just a simple biochemical explanation, therefore, really just a hormonal reaction?
Either way, she enjoyed the moment and left the melancholy thoughts behind her.

And so, they clung to each other — their cosmic family — finding solace in shared laughter, whispered confessions, and the distant promise of Mars.

Chapter 3: Lecture Sessions

As previously described, during the long flight from Earth to Mars, the crew has an organized program to pass time. One of the jeur-fixe dates are the lecture sessions.

Destination: Excursion into Volcanology

Today it is Emily's turn to give her geological view on the destination.

"Please fasten your seatbelt, our flight's destination will be Cydonia Mensae", Emily started the lecture.

"Doesn't this sound like a seaside resort, does it? I can't wait to enjoy sun, beach, drinks and palm trees with background Caribbean music", Klaus interjected.

"I must disappoint you about this, Klaus", Emily answered. "The Cydonia region on Mars is located in the planet's northern hemisphere, within the transition zone between the heavily cratered southern highlands and the smoother northern plains."

"Where does the name Cydonia come from, by the way?", Ivan asked.

Emily stopped for a moment and uttered: "Um, er…"

Klaus sprang to help, as he had enjoyed a classical language education at high school:
"The name "Cydonia" originates from the ancient Greek word for the city of Kydonia (modern-day Chania) on the island of Crete. In

Greek mythology, Kydonia was associated with a type of fruit that later became known as the quince."

Emily continued slightly impressed with a reddish color flush in her face:"However, this region is characterized by mesas (flat-topped hills with steep sides) and buttes (similar to mesas but smaller). For example, buttes are also found on Earth in Monument Valley, Utah, and have been often used for primitive American Western movie sets."

"Your haughty tone shows a kind of disrespect to our cultural heritage", Commander Harris said a little tarnished in honor.

"Well, the British history is just much more profound and insignificantly older, isn't it?", Emily retorted.

"I protest", injected Wei, "China has definitely the oldest and richest cultural history among all of us here."

"Yeah, both of you are right. Don't mind, keep going on", Commander Harris nodded towards Emily.

"These formations in the Cydonia region are believed to have been shaped by erosion caused by wind, water, and possibly volcanic activity", Emily continued her lecture. "The region of interest for our mission is the following volcano and its surroundings", she projected the following picture to the wall.

Sophie awakened from a sleepy condition and asked:
"How can you be so sure that this is a volcano and not an impact crater by a meteor?"

"This is a very good question indeed", Emily responded. She went on to say:
"In geology, we first look at shape and symmetry:
On the one hand volcanoes often have a conical or shield-like shape with gentle slopes. They have a central opening or crater called a summit crater. On the other hand impact craters typically have a circular shape with sharp, often elevated rims and may have a central

mountain or central rise inside, created by the rebound effects of the impact.”

“Well, that is plausible. So this is a volcano”, Sophie responded.

“Not so quick because we also have to look at the surrounding material”, Emily lectured her. “The surroundings of volcanoes often show solidified lava flows and pyroclastic deposits. These materials can be distributed radially around the volcano. Ejecta blankets and secondary craters formed by ejected material are often found around impact craters. This material is usually chaotic and distributed in concentric rings around the crater.”

With a mischievous look, Klaus threw in another question:
“But you sure would have a third aspect as "three things are charming", wouldn’t you?”

“Klaus, admit it, you secretly skipped your chemistry and biology lectures to study geology”, she winked her eyes at him.

Klaus winked back at her. She almost had the feeling that he was flirting. But she was probably wrong.

Emily collected herself again, presented another colorful picture of the site and began to recite again:
“Well, there is the spectroscopy: Spectral analysis can provide information about the mineralogical composition of the surface. Volcanoes often show evidence of volcanic rocks such as basalt, while impact craters may show a wider range of materials exposed by the impact. By combining these methods, scientists can precisely determine whether a particular feature on Mars is of volcanic origin or was formed by a meteorite impact.”
She continued to show another split picture of three craters.

Emily continued pointing at the left crater first:
"Olympus Mons: A large shield volcano with a height of about 22 km...", she stopped to continue with an emphasis: "13.7 miles for the American".

"Yeah, yeah, we always get this for the Mars Climate Orbiter incident from 1999", Commander Harris replied annoyed.
The Orbiter was destroyed due to a unit conversion error between the spacecraft's software teams. Specifically, the navigation team used metric units (newton-seconds) for calculations, while the contractorused imperial units (pound-seconds). This discrepancy caused the spacecraft to enter Mars' atmosphere at a much lower altitude than planned.

Emily smiled smiled triumphantly, although she had to admit to herself that the British also refused to adopt the metric system for a long time. She continued:
"And Olympus Mons has a broad, shallow caldera at the top. The shape and lava flows are typical of volcanic activity."

Then she pointed to the picture in the middle explaining:
"In contrast Gale crater: An impact crater with a central mountain (Mount Sharp) and sharp, terraced rims, typical of impact structures."

"Got it", Klaus interjected, "but what is the difference between the crater in the middle picture and the one on the right?"

"You're really impatient, Klaus!", Emily replied smiling. "This is neither a volcano nor an impact crater, but a pingo. Pingos are ice-cored hills formed in permafrost regions due to the upward movement and freezing of groundwater. One of the areas where pingo-like features have been identified is Utopia Planitia, a large plain in the northern hemisphere of Mars."

"But we are not here for volcanoes only", Ivan murmered. "Otherwise Mrs. Li wouldn't be sitting here, right?"

Wei took this as an opportunity to speak:
"Sure, it is about the renewed speculation of prehistoric ruins of a civilization with pyramids and the "Face on Mars" based on new satellite and land probe imaging data. Obviously we have been deceived for a very long time to face the unwanted reality. Fact is that these novel findings are not just simple random stone or mountain formation."

Klaus smiled enthusiastically at Wei, which did not go unnoticed by Emily. She could not explain why she was so much interested in the nonverbal interaction between Klaus and Wei, but somehow she disliked it. What is wrong with her? A feeling of grudge and grumble was inside her.

Emily felt compelled to take back the sceptre of the lecture:
"As a geologist, I have to say that the mystery of Cydonia Mensae and the "Martian Face" illustrates the human tendency to interpret something into unclear visual data, a phenomenon known as pareidolia. While initial images from the Viking 1 orbiter in 1976 fueled imaginations and speculations, subsequent high-resolution imaging and

scientific analysis have provided a clear understanding of the natural geological processes at work in the region."

"Alright, it is late already. Thank you for the deep look inside geology and your British charm. Tomorrow Wei will give us a lecture on pyramids and ancient cultures. I am curious how Wei will broaden our horizons. Good night!" When Commander Harris said this, he directly made his way to his quarters.
He looked tired indeed. Today's routine system checks have been tough and tiresome for everyone. So everybody else did not make a fuss about and rapidly headed for their quarters, too.
Emily tried to catch a glimpse of Klaus, but he was already focused on his way to bed.
Sophie bumped in to Ivan when getting up from their chairs. Both of them smiled with a little spark in the eye. Gentleman-like Ivan let Sophie pass by first. Sophie turned around again with a seductive look before heading purposefully to her bunk. Ivan felt happy, a feeling he had yearned for a very long time.

Pyramids

The next evening was the announced lecture by Wei. The crew member gathered to listen to her presentation.
Emily fooled herself to think that she was indifferent on Klaus's and Wei's interaction. However, she deliberately sat opposite from Klaus just to scrutinize any reactions between them.
Sophie again sat beside Ivan. She accidentally touched his arm when she sat down. With a shy look, she said a quick "Pardon!".
Ivan whispered to her:"Now we're bumping into each other again. Are we magnetically charged?"

Ivan winked charmingly in Sophie's direction, but discreetly so that the other crew members wouldn't notice. She winked back secretly and he moistened his lips. There was a slight crackle between them.

Wei started her lecture as follows:
"The pyramids, particularly those of ancient Egypt, stand as monumental achievements in human history, representing the zenith of architectural, engineering, and organizational skills of early civilizations. These massive stone structures, primarily built as tombs for pharaohs and other significant figures, have fascinated historians, archaeologists, and tourists for centuries."

Wei showed the first picture to the audience of a classical Egyptian pyramid.

Klaus suddenly asked:
"What do we actually know more about the purpose and meaning of a pyramid now?"

Wei turned to address Klaus directly:
"We now think that the primary purpose of the pyramids was to serve as tombs for pharaohs and elite members of society. They were believed to be the dwelling places for the afterlife, ensuring the deceased's safe passage and immortality. The pyramids were part of larger complexes that included temples, smaller pyramids for queens, and mastabas (tomb structures) for nobles, all designed to support the pharaoh's journey in the afterlife."

Klaus commented:
"Well, that be something to find the key to longevity and maybe immortality."

Ivan turned to Klaus and agreed:
"Yes, the medicine on lifespan is still challenging. Can you give us a
lecture tomorrow on your scientific achievement, Klaus?"

Klaus chuckled:
"Sure, if you won't die of boredom then and think that I am qualified
enough because I have not won a Nobel Prize yet."

Emily smiled over to Klaus. She liked Klaus's humor.

Commander Harris intervened as the host:
"Please continue Wei."

Wei stated the following:
"The interior of the pyramids was often decorated with intricate carvings and texts from the Book of the Dead, meant to guide the deceased through the afterlife. The burial chambers contained the pharaoh's sarcophagus and various grave goods, including jewelry, food, and artifacts, intended to provide for the king in the next world."

"Isn't the theory of a tomb chamber in Egyptian pyramids questioned as the pharaohs' tombs have been found in the Valley of Kings nearby Luxor?", Klaus interjected.

Emily gloated about Klaus's comment to Wei.

Wei replied coolly and calmly:
"The theory that the pyramids were built as tombs for pharaohs is not necessarily wrong, even though many pharaohs from later periods were buried in the Valley of the Kings near Luxor. Understanding this requires a recognition of the historical development of Egyptian funerary practices and the evolution of royal tomb construction. But that would go beyond the scope of this session and distract from what I'm trying to get at in the first place."

Klaus shrugged his shoulders. Ultimately, it was not his intention to doubt Wei's competence or to try to outdo her. But he wasn't worried about Wei. Above all, he even had to secretly admit to himself that he found the character of a feisty woman quite attractive.

But he wasn't here on a mission to date women, he was completely dedicated to science. At least that's what he told himself as self-protection or armor. Or should he also allow feelings? Wouldn't that be tantamount to weakness?

Klaus' rambling thoughts were cut short when Wei raised her voice again: "Quiz question: What do we see here?"

She projected the next slide.

Ivan commented immediately:

"I like the architecture of this pyramid."

Wei corrected Ivan:
"Wrong, this is a ziggurat, not a pyramid!"

"So what is the difference then?" Ivan retorted.

Wei explained:
"Ziggurats are distinct from other ancient structures due to their unique, stepped design. Unlike the smooth-sided pyramids of Egypt, ziggurats are built with a series of successively smaller platforms stacked upon one another, creating a terraced appearance.
The ziggurats built in the ancient cities of Mesopotamia, particularly in modern-day Iraq and Iran, are stepped pyramids consisting of a series of stacked platforms.
The base of a ziggurat is typically rectangular or square, with each successive level receding inward, forming a stepped pyramid. The construction of a ziggurat involved the use of sun-dried mud bricks for the core structure, while the exterior was often faced with baked bricks to protect against the elements. These bricks were held together with bitumen, a naturally occurring tar-like substance that provided additional waterproofing. These structures were built in the ancient cities of Mesopotamia, particularly in modern-day Iraq and Iran, and primarily had a religious function. Each city had a ziggurat, which served as a temple for the city deity. The most famous of these is the ziggurat of Ur, which was dedicated to the moon god Nanna. The ziggurats symbolized the sacred mountain, which was regarded as the connection between heaven and earth. These buildings were not only religious centers, but also places of social and political power. The priests who administered the ziggurats played a central role in the administration of the city-states. The monumental ziggurats served as visible signs of the city's divine support and prosperity."

Now Wei continued her lecture with the next slide.

"I guess, this is another ziggurat then, right?" Ivan brought forward. Sophie tugged on Ivan's arm.

Wei smiled and answered:
"Wrong again, Ivan. This is a Mayan pyramid.
In Mesoamerica, particularly in the Mayan and Aztec cultures, pyramids were also built that had both religious and political functions. These pyramids, such as those in the Mayan city of Chichen Itza or the Aztec pyramid of Tenochtitlán, were often temple platforms on which rituals and offerings were made to the gods.

The Mesoamerican pyramids were often linked to astronomical and calendrical considerations. They served as observatories and their orientation and structure were strongly influenced by the movements of the celestial bodies. The pyramids symbolized sacred geography and the cosmic mountain that represented the world order."

With a slight hesitation, Wei presented her final slide.

She couldn't refrain from making a pointed remark directed at Emily, as she has not forgotten the hostile comment and look from her during yesterday's lecture:
"Just to take the wind out of the sails of inveterate geologists, the picture is self-explanatory, I think."

Emily made a fiendish look at Wei.
What was it about them?
Is it just a rivalry in science or something else?
But Emily had not the time to think over because she, as all the others in the room, have been shocked what they have been presented with the following slide: A five-sided pyramid on Mars with two moons in the sky.

A murmur went through the room.

Sophie groaned: "Mon dieu!" and Klaus almost simultaneously said: "Mein Gott!"

"Yes, this is no fake, this is a confirmed image of a Martian pyramid indeed! The picture has been taken by the recent Chinese land probe. The image was given the highest level of confidentiality — top secret! Despite political differences between our governments, the international space exploration works well. It has been agreed at government level to keep the public out of these new discoveries."

Klaus was the first to collect himself and asked:
"Doesn't this bear some resemblance to the ancient Egyptian pyramids?"

Emily nodded to Klaus as if she wanted to give her support to him, although he definitely wouldn't need that.

Wei replied:
"True, but there is a significant difference to that. The Martian pyramid is five-sided, a thing which is unheard of for comparable architecture on Earth. Moreover, we find on the distorted image a kind of hieroglyphical writing at the outside. The image quality is too low to get a clear vision for interpretation."

Wei paused for a few seconds to begin with the next sentence:
"Now you all know what I am here for."

Everybody was eager to hear more from here. You could have heard a needle drop.

After a short break of five seconds everyone applauded. Even Emily could not refuse to do so.

Commander Harris stood up and made a warning in front of his crew:
"Uncle Sam has given me the orders to maintain confidentiality and give you information on a need-to-know basis."

"Uncle Sam? Why haven't we Europeans be informed about this?", Emily said bewildered.

"Europeans? Since when do the English consider themselves Europeans? You are always opportunist and double-minded people. You could never make up mind to be the 51st state or belong to Europe", Sophie said in an annoyed tone.

Klaus ran inroads for his European counterpart and said,
"Be that as it may, what's more important, why haven't we be informed about this from the beginning? I agree with Emily, Europeans one or another, they are allowed to pay a lot of money, but are not in charge anytime. Obviously we are only regarded as water carriers here."

When Klaus brought this "I agree with Emily", another red flush came into Emily's face, as she has experienced yesterday.

Now Commander Harris felt obliged to provide additional information:
"I can fully understand your discomfort to this situation. However, all what has been and will be said here is strictly classified. You are embargoed to provide any information to your relatives and friends at home. According to your personal records, nobody of you is married or has any children, therefore the risk of a leak of information is minimal."

"Under whose authority you issue you a gag order on us? According to my information you don't have any jurisdiction here", Ivan reacted, who has been noticeable silent up until now.

"Don't be hypocritical, Ivan", Klaus said. "Otherwise you wouldn't have given your remark on Wei's role during Emily's lecture yesterday."
And he did it again, Emily's name came through Klaus's lips.
Emily was thrilled.

"So admit it, Ivan. You have been previously informed through your intelligence service", Klaus continued.

"Not at all, it was just simple logic" Ivan retorted. Klaus left this uncommented, but gave it a wry smile.

Now Commander Harris took the floor again:
"Alright, I owe you an explanation. The US and Chinese government had a secret agreement not to reveal any specific information about the true objectives of this mission, up until it is inevitable. Yes, this point has reached now. And I do rephrase my wording now: I apologize to you all. I would kindly ask you not to provide anything to the outside world yet. We should give a carefully considered statement. Any whistleblowing may do harm to us, to mission control and to our governments who will have to cope with a new delicate situation. Because nobody can imagine the effect on our home planet: religious world views collapse, riots break out, governments are toppled and societies may end up in chaos. Therefore, we bear very great responsibility. Keep in mind about the consequences."

It was late again and everybody directly headed for their quarters after a short farewell. There was not even room left for flirting signals between Ivan and Sophie or between Klaus and Emily or Wei respectively this time. This groundbreaking lecture and the following discussion got to everybody. Some suffered from sleep disorder for the upcoming night. There was too much new information, which needed to be processed in their brains. For some, it is the shaking of the world and religious view, in particular for Catholic Sophie. When the divine creation story is called into question, this is a significant problem for Catholics and believers of many other religious denominations.

Also the legal confrontation was confusing to most of them. According to the Outer Space Treaty (OST) of 1967, which has been ratified by all major spacefaring countries, outer space, including Mars, is not subject to national appropriation by any means and states would retain jurisdiction and control over their registered space objects and personnel. Even though Commander Harris was the commander to this mission, the responsibility lies with the nations and cannot be overruled by another, actually.

However, who is really in charge here, and the omnipresent secrecy of information have created an atmosphere of mistrust. The vase was cracked and nobody knew whether it could be repaired and whether team building could be restored.

Hieroglyphs

The next day, crew members worked in an automode until the time of the evening lecture meeting.

Despite the emotional coolness in the aisles of the spacecraft, the flames of affection regained and kept flickering between Ivan and Sophie, as well as from Emily's and Wei's side with regard to Klaus, but not from Klaus's direction so far.

When everybody had taken their seats, Commander Harris started with the following declaration:
"Dear fellows, after yesterday's revelation and the critical discussion, I once again want to express my deepest apologies.

To reinstate trust with you all, I have talked to Wei earlier, and we have come to the conclusion to show you the whole picture. I mean, you get to know all now, I really mean "all", no secrets left out.
"I fully understand your concerns, and you may have your doubts about me, about each other, and my leadership. You may question

my orders now. But what is at stake here is for a greater purpose and is much more than any of you can ever imagine. Even though we know each other for a rather short time, I would personally trust each of you with my life. Therefore, I would just like to ask you to show a little faith"(for insiders, he had quoted with the last few sentences a legendary scifi figure who resembled him in many ways)."

Commander Harris made a short break to restart his speech:
"Klaus, unfortunately I will have to ask you to take a raincheck with your lecture on longevity tonight because we are willing to wipe the slate clean, to give us all a fresh start."

Klaus nodded in understanding and said:
"No problem at all. I can hardly wait to find out what else has been left behind the mountain. Let's begin!"

Commander Harris turned to Wei and opened his hand to show her the way to the speaker's desk:
"Please! Go on, Wei!"

Wei gasped and started with her words:

"My dear companions, my dear friends. Yes, we have encountered a difficult situation. However, it may be more challenging for all of us soon and, therefore I hope that issues can be settled ASAP because we really don't have time for inner conflicts here."

Sophie clandestinely grapped Ivan's hand, and he let her hand have its way. Ivan felt that Sophie was afraid, and she was looking for a protection of sorts.

"Thanks to the help of German optical technology", Wei smiled over to Klaus who benevolently responded with a nodding and smiling, something which remained not unnoticed through Emily's eagle eyes, "we have been able to visualize an enhanced image of the glyphs on these reconstructed pictures."

Klaus's background with the benefits of a classical education helped him to recognize and categorize the inscription immediately, and thus, he rapidly uttered:
"This looks familiar to me with cuneiform writings."

Wei grinned and felt a kind of mutual worship through Klaus's comments now.
She answered accordingly:
"Yes and no. I know how far-fetched it may appear, but as a matter of fact, the Martian inscription has partly a relationship to Sumerian cuneiform writings, but also ancient Egyptian hieroglyphs. My research team has pondered for a very long time for an appropriate translation."

Now she wrote several characters and/or hieroglyphs on the digital blackboard and she continued her monologue:
"The relationship between the Sumerian and Egyptian languages is an interesting topic in historical linguistics, although the two languages are not directly related. Both Sumerian and Egyptian are among the earliest known written languages, with their own unique writing systems and linguistic characteristics. Here's a detailed look at their relationship and key features:
Sumerian is a language isolate, meaning it has no known relatives and does not belong to any language family. It was spoken in ancient Mesopotamia, in the region corresponding to modern-day southern Iraq. In contrast, Egyptian belongs to the Afro-Asiatic language family, specifically the branch known as the Egyptian languages. This family also includes Semitic languages like Arabic and Hebrew, Berber, Cushitic, and Chadic languages. Egyptian was spoken in ancient Egypt.

The Sumerians developed cuneiform script, one of the earliest writing systems, around 3500-3000 BC. It involved the use of a stylus to make wedge-shaped marks on clay tablets.
The ancient Egyptians developed hieroglyphic writing around the same time period. Hieroglyphs are pictorial symbols that were carved on monuments and written on papyrus.
Linguistic characteristics are that Sumerian is agglutinative, whereas Egyptian is…"

Commander Harris interrupted Wei:
"Wei, please make it understandable to everybody here and come to the point."
Wei has been convinced that her report was proper for an expert audience of linguists, but not for a multinational astronaut crew with different academic background. Therefore, she skipped to the key hieroglyphs and started up to explain:
"There are repeatedly found the three Martian hieroglyphs which bear some resemblance with the following words from Sumerian and ancient Egyptian language:

1. The Djed ⚱ is an ancient Egyptian hieroglyph. The Djed pillar's visual representation typically consists of a vertical column with four horizontal bars at the top, resembling a stylized tree or pillar with a series of crossbars."

Sophie interjected:
"From the engineers view, this looks to me much like a pylon."

Wei answered and continued:
"While the visual similarity between the Djed pillar and a telegraph pylon can be noted, there is no historical or archaeo-

logical evidence to support the claim that the ancient Egyptians intended the Djed to represent a technological device. The traditional and widely accepted understanding is that the Djed pillar is a religious symbol deeply embedded in the mythological and cultural framework of ancient Egypt. The Djed pillar symbolizes the concept of stability and strength, and is often interpreted as a representation of the spine of the god Osiris, who is associated with resurrection in the afterlife and eternal life. Moreover, it symbolizes the renewal of the king's power and the stability of the universe.

The pendant to the Djed hieroglyph in Sumerian culture, representing stability, strength, and endurance, can be seen in the

"Me" concept, symbolized by the cuneiform sign ⌐ . The "Me" were fundamental decrees or divine principles that governed all aspects of existence, including the natural world, human society, and religious practices. These principles were believed to be bestowed by the gods and were intrinsic to maintaining order and stability in the universe. An example from Sumerian mythology highlighting the importance of the "Me" is the myth of Inanna and Enki, where Inanna, the goddess of love and war, travels to the city of Eridu to receive the "Me" from Enki, the god of wisdom. This myth underscores the significance of these divine principles in maintaining cosmic and social order.

While the Djed pillar and the "Me" concept are from two distinct ancient cultures, they both symbolize the importance of stability, continuity, and divine order in their respective mythologies and worldviews.

2. This Djet hieroglyph ⎕ depicts a human arm holding a sun-
    disk, which symbolizes the concept of a period or moment. It
    can be used in the context of time-related words such as
    "hour" or "moment." The Sumerian term "ĝeš" ⬦ can rep-
    resent the concept of time or cycles. This is also in accord-
    ance with the latest view of time. Although we are used to
    modern physics and language to observe the flow of time in a
    linear way, the cyclic aspect seems to be more resourceful.
    Thus, some cultures depicted time in a cyclic manner and not
    from α to Ω."

Klaus couldn't hesitate to comment:
"So you refer to the "wheel of time" as we originally have found
this in Mayan culture or on thangkas in Tibet or should I rather
say China?"

Even though Wei found strong sympathy with Klaus, the last
comment annoyed her a bit because she considered this an of-
fence or insult by the German.

However, Emily was secretly pleased that this criticism was being
leveled against Wei by Klaus.

Wei, who derived from a diplomatic family and was used to political provocation, continued with the listing of the hieroglyphs
and said nonchalantly:"Western people cannot understand China
— fullstop.

3. Finally, the Netjer hieroglyph represents the concept of a deity or god in ancient Egyptian writing. It is often used as a determinative or classifier placed after the names of gods and goddesses in hieroglyphic texts to indicate their divine sta-tus. The symbol depicts a seated figure with uplifted arms, emphasizing the divine nature and authority of the subject. In the cuneiform script, an eight-pointed star is its symbol, which is used as the determinative Dingir/Diĝir.”

Sophie has raised the following precarious question:“What is actually the connection between the speed of light and the coordinates of the pyramids in Giza?”

Wei replied soberly:“The supposed connection between the speed of light in a vacuum, which is approximately 299,792,458 meters per second and the geographic coordinates of the Great Pyramid of Giza (29.9792° N) is likely a coincidence and not an indication of ancient scientific knowledge or intentional design. While it is an interesting numerical curiosity, there is no credible evidence to support the idea that the ancient Egyptians designed the pyramids with this knowledge in mind.“

Now it was Commander Harris’s turn to moderate and conclude: “Once we have landed, we will have to watch out for alien artifacts and technology, which be Emily’s and Sophie’s job. In addition, we also have to be prepared to encounter even biological lifeforms, which will the special task for Klaus and Ivan. Wei will give you all the hand with cryptography deciphering. There will be risks for the safety of the crew, but also the chance to make the biggest discovery of mankind after the sailing to the New World by explorer and navigator Christopher Columbus."

The mood in the team improved significantly after the presentation, even if Sophie's fears are currently predominant.

Longevity

Today's daily routine went off without a hitch. However, yesterday's lecture was a liberating blow. The crew seemed more relaxed and developed trust and self-confidence among themselves to face the new challenges.

Nevertheless, everyone was now looking forward to Klaus' lecture. Even though he probably wouldn't contribute much to the imminent mission on the red planet, the lecture promised to be a welcome distraction.

Klaus stepped forward and spoke in a deep, sonorous voice, using a unique voice modulation and emphasis on the individual words. One could almost have thought that a theater actor had been lost in the professor. No wonder that both Wei and Emily fell for him. He began with stress on the onomatopoetic word "longevity":

"Longevity, the duration of an individual's life, has been a focal point of human interest for centuries. Advances in medicine, technology, and lifestyle have significantly increased average lifespans in modern societies. Among the numerous factors contributing to longevity, natural products — derived from plants, animals, and minerals — play a crucial role due to their potential health benefits. These natural products, encompassing a range of substances such as herbs, dietary supplements, and functional foods, have been shown to influence aging processes and promote a healthier, longer life."

Klaus paused for a few seconds to continue:
"Natural products can influence longevity through various mechanisms. These include antioxidative properties, anti-inflammatory effects, enhancement of cellular repair mechanisms, and modulation of metabolic pathways."
Klaus continue to present slides with pictures from red wine, herbs and fish to demonstrate their potential benefits in both animal and human studies. He gained particular attention from Wei when he began to explain Chinese characters referring to Jiagulan 绞股蓝 or Xiancao 仙草 as the "herb of immortality". Wei's ice was finally broken, she has literally melted away. Klaus expressed so much devotion and appreciation for Chinese culture and traditional Chinese medicine:
"Jiaogulan (Gynostemma pentaphyllum), often referred to as "Southern Ginseng" or the "Herb of Immortality," is a climbing vine native to China and other parts of Asia. For centuries, it has been used in traditional Chinese medicine for its reputed health benefits, including promoting longevity. For several years, scientific research has begun to explore the mechanisms behind Jiaogulan's effects, providing evidence that supports its potential as an herb for enhancing lifespan and overall health."

Wei cherished strong hopes that she will have a chance on this mission to come closer to Klaus, but she knew that she was not the only competitor in this game looking shortly over to Emily.

Klaus ended his lecture with the following concluding remarks:
"However, some national laws prevent the use of food supplements and teas. Furthermore, the practical considerations of quality, dosage,

bioavailability, and interactions must be carefully managed to maximize their benefits and minimize risks. As research in this field advances, natural products may become increasingly integral to strategies aimed at promoting longer, healthier lives."

Everyone in the room was gripped by the possibilities of modern science. Soon there were no longer any limits to how old a person could live. And it wasn't just about living longer, but also about quality of life.

Ivan also repeatedly agreed with the advances in medicine in recent years. Ultimately, this has also contributed to the fact that a mission like the one they are currently carrying out is only possible in the first place due to the mental and physical exertions.

Commander Harris thanked Klaus and wished everyone a good night's sleep. He was pleased that the harmony in the crew and the team spirit had been restored.

One thing was clear, Wei would have very special dreams that night. She was deeply touched because she had rarely experienced a Westerner dealing with her culture with such empathy and understanding. But it was not only the rational, intellectual level that touched her deeply, some would call it sapiosexual attraction, it was also emotionally moving. Something had happened inside her that she, as a mind-controlled woman who had won high-performance intelligence competitions with an IQ of 160, could no longer control. She had never experienced such a feeling before and it even frightened her in a way, because she was no longer herself. She had grown up with unconditional self-discipline and was constantly taught this in her upbringing, whether at home with her family or at school.

But she wasn't the only one who was inwardly moved.

Emily was also fascinated by Klaus's talk. Although, like Wei, she is undoubtedly a scientist through and through, Emily was also touched inside. It wasn't so much the content of the lecture, but the meta-level. Klaus' gestures and facial expressions, the vibrations of his deep, warm voice that somehow turned her on. Emily longed for any favorable opportunity to get closer to Klaus. But there was always the fear of being rejected by him. She definitely had a different character to Sophie, who as a Frenchwoman had a carefree demeanor and sex appeal. Emily just can't explain away her British ancestry. British women have a more reserved character compared to French-women, but this can also spoil their chances of finding a partner.

In any case, Emily will have intense dreams the next night for sure, if she can fall asleep at all, because she has to think about Klaus all the time. Whether this is beneficial for her health and longevity, as mentioned in Klaus' talk, remains to be seen.

Chapter 4: Love and Rivalry

The First Kiss

The spaceflight from Earth to Mars was a symphony of anticipation and isolation. The six astronauts — each a note in this cosmic composition —— orbited the void, their hearts echoing the thrum of the spacecraft's engines.

Sophie sat by the observation window, her breath fogging the glass. Earth, a distant blue gem, receded behind them. Ivan approached, his footsteps silent in the low gravity.

"Beautiful, isn't it?" Ivan said, his Russian accent soft. His brown eyes held galaxies within.

Sophie tore her gaze from the stars. "Yes. But it's also terrifying. We're hurtling through space, leaving everything we know."

Ivan leaned closer, their breaths mingling. "Sometimes fear and wonder are two sides of the same comet."

She laughed — a fragile sound in the sterile cabin. "Comets burn up. Do you think we'll burn up too?"

He reached for her hand, their fingers entwining. "Not if we find our own constellations."

And so, in the quiet of the interplanetary night, they shared secrets. Sophie spoke of her childhood dreams — of stardust and ancient mysteries. Ivan confessed his fear of forgetting Earth's scent — the damp forests, the salt of the sea.

As Mars loomed ahead, Sophie's heart raced. Ivan's lips were inches away, and the universe held its breath. She tasted the tang of recycled air, felt the hum of the ship against her skin.

"Will we survive this?" she whispered.

Ivan's kiss was an answer - an ignition of longing and possibility. Their lips met, and time folded in on itself. Earth, Mars, and all the forgotten worlds spun around them.

When they broke apart, Sophie's cheeks flushed. "We're still hurt-ling," she said.

"But now," Ivan replied, "we're hurtling together."

And so, amidst the constellations and the weightlessness, Sophie and Ivan found their orbit - a trajectory that defied gravity and logic. Love, like the cosmos, knew no bounds.

The spacecraft hummed through the interplanetary void, its metal walls cocooning the crew in a fragile bubble of existence. Sophie and Ivan's love had become a secret whispered between star charts and ration packets. But secrets, like orbits, had a way of shifting.

Ivan and Sophie mastered the art of discretion at the workplace. They avoided lingering glances, whispered conversations, and lunchtime rendezvous. No stolen kisses in the supply closet - only professional camaraderie.

Sophie slipped cryptic notes into Ivan's pocket during team meetings. A folded paper with a heart drawn in the corner - a silent promise.

They met at the coffee machine, exchanging coded smiles. The warmth of the cup mirrored the warmth of their hidden love. Sophie and Ivan lingered, the shared secret in their eyes.

The crew adjusted. Some smiled knowingly; others raised eyebrows. Wei, always observant, winked at Sophie.

Ivan and Sophie's love became an open secret - a comet streaking across the mission logs.

Sophie and Ivan found solace in the ship's observatory - a small chamber with a domed ceiling that simulated the night sky. Stars blinked into existence, their constellations familiar yet distant. Sophie traced Orion's belt, her finger brushing imaginary stardust.

Ivan stood beside her, his breath visible in the chilled air. "You know," he said, "the ancients believed that stars were souls. Each one a story waiting to be told."

Sophie leaned closer. "What's our story, Ivan?"

He hesitated, then took her hand. "Our story? It's written in the way your eyes light up when you decode engineering algorithms. It's in the way I memorize the curve of your smile during zero-gravity maneuvers."

Sophie's heart raced. "But nobody knows."

"Exactly." Ivan's gaze held hers. "Our love is a comet — a celestial secret. But comets burn brightest when they're closest to the sun."

Sophie's eyes shimmered like the stars above. "So, what happens when we get too close?"

Ivan smiled softly. "Then we shine for all to see, even if it's just for a fleeting moment. Because those moments, Sophie, are what make the universe beautiful."

She sighed, a mixture of contentment and longing. "I've always wondered about the future, about what's next."

Ivan gently brushed a strand of hair from her face. "The future is a mystery, like the stars we chart. But here, now, with you, I know it's a journey worth taking."

Sophie leaned her head on Ivan's shoulder, the two of them standing together, surrounded by the infinite cosmos. The stars in the observatory twinkled brightly, reflecting their silent promises and dreams. The silence was comforting, a stark contrast to the bustling life of the ship.

"What do you think lies out there?" Sophie whispered, eyes closed, imagining the vastness beyond their ship.

"Possibilities," Ivan replied softly. "New worlds, new experiences. But no matter where we go or what we find, as long as we have each other, we'll always have a home."

Sophie nodded, feeling the truth in his words. "Promise me we'll always chase the stars together?"

Ivan pressed a gentle kiss on her forehead. "Always, Sophie. Always."

As they stood there, entwined in each other's embrace, the simulated stars continued to shine, witnessing their vow. The universe outside, vast and enigmatic, awaited their exploration. But in that moment, in their private observatory under a digital night sky, they found a universe within each other.

The Unveiling Moment

One day, as the crew gathered for a routine briefing, Sophie's hand brushed Ivan's under the table. Their fingers entwined, and the room blurred around them. Commander Harris droned on about Martian soil samples, but Sophie only heard the rush of blood in her ears.

Wei leaned over. "Sophie," she whispered, "your secret is safe with me. Love is a universal language."

Sophie blushed. "How did you —"

Wei winked. "I've seen the way you two share protein bars. It's not rocket science."

And then, during a simulated emergency drill, Ivan's voice crackled over the intercom. "Sophie, meet me in the observatory."

She floated there, heart pounding, as Ivan entered. The stars shimmered above them — their silent witnesses.

"Ivan," Sophie said, "what if someone finds out?"

He cupped her face. "Then we'll be a binary star system — a pair that dances across the cosmos."

"Ivan," she whispered, "I love you."

His hand brushed hers. "And I love you."

And there, beneath the simulated constellations, Ivan kissed her. Sophie clung to him, her heart spiraling into infinity.

As they emerged from the observatory, the crew stared. Sophie raised an eyebrow.

Commander Harris noticed — the way their fingers lingered, the shared secret in their eyes.

"Sophie," he said, voice stern, "we need honesty among the crew."

Sophie hesitated, then nodded. "We're together."

"Well," she said, "I guess we've found our Martian romance."

Emily grinned. "It's like "Romeo and Juliet" meets "The Martian"."

Wei observed them keenly. She'd seen enough rom-coms to know how this played out. "Love is like a Martian dust storm," she mused. "Unpredictable and messy."

And Commander Harris? He sighed. "As long as it doesn't interfere with our mission."

Sophie's lips met Ivan's — a kiss that transcended time and space. Their souls merged across the void, intertwining like constellations. The machine hummed, amplifying their emotions — their desire, their love. Sophie and Ivan's love story became part of the ship's folklore — a whispered legend among the stars.

Love was in the air, but not only for them both, though…

Celestial Chemistry

Emily watched Sophie and Ivan from across the lab. Their laughter echoed through the chamber as they huddled over technical protocol texts. The way Sophie's hand brushed against Ivan's — Emily's heart clenched. She had always been drawn to Klaus, the stoic German scientist, but now Wei threatened to steal his attention.

Emily couldn't let Wei win Klaus's heart. She had spent years studying the geology of distant planets, but now her own heart was a rocky terrain. Klaus was brilliant, enigmatic, and infuriatingly focused on scientific tasks.

One night, as they worked side by side, Emily blurted out, "Klaus, do you believe in destiny?"

Klaus looked up from his notes. "Destiny?"

Emily's voice trembled. "Maybe we're meant to be here," she said. "Not just for science, but for something more."

Klaus noticed Emily's attempt to get closer. "Emily," he said, "we're here for a reason. The pyramid holds answers beyond our wildest dreams."

Emily clenched her fists. "I know," she replied. "But sometimes, Klaus, love is the greatest mystery of all."

Emily watched, torn between jealousy and awe. Klaus stepped closer, his gaze fixed on Sophie and Ivan. "Emily," he said softly, "sometimes love is the greatest discovery of all."

Stellar Conversations

The observation deck became their sanctuary — a place where starlight painted their skin and the hum of the ship faded into the background. Emily leaned against the transparent viewport, her eyes fixed on the distant pinpricks of light. Klaus stood beside her, his analytical mind momentarily silenced by the vastness of space."Do you ever wonder," Emily began, her voice soft, "what lies beyond the stars? What secrets the universe keeps hidden?"

Klaus had the feeling that Emily was teasing him a little with this question. He studied her profile — the curve of her jaw, the freckles dusting her cheeks. "I wonder," he admitted. "But I've always believed that answers lie in equations, in data. Not in the poetry of the cosmos."

"Ah, but poetry can unlock truths too," Emily countered. "The way a nebula swirls, the birth and death of stars — it's all part of a grand narrative."

"Narratives don't fuel rockets." Klaus said, but there was a hint of curiosity in his eyes. "What's your favorite constellation, Emily?"

She grinned. "Orion. The Hunter. It's like a cosmic warrior, forever chasing the Pleiades across the sky."

"And you?" Emily asked, turning the question back on him.

Klaus hesitated. "Cassiopeia," he said finally. "The Queen. She defied the gods and paid the price. A cautionary tale."

"Or perhaps a tale of courage," Emily mused. "To challenge fate, to reach for the unreachable."

They stood there, two scientists with hearts as vast as the universe. Emily's fingers brushed Klaus's, and he didn't pull away. "Maybe," he said, "we're all chasing our own constellations — our own truths."

"And what's your truth, Klaus Müller?" Emily whispered.

He leaned closer, his breath warm against her ear. "That the cosmos is more than equations," he murmured. "That sometimes, love defies gravity."

Forbidden Moments

The ship's corridors were dimly lit, the hum of machinery a constant companion. Emily and Klaus found solace in these hidden spaces — their stolen moments away from prying eyes. They'd meet after their shifts, their hearts racing as they leaned against the cold metal walls.

"Klaus," Emily whispered, her breath warm against his cheek. "We can't keep doing this."

He pulled her closer, his analytical mind silenced by desire. "I know," he murmured. "But love defies logic, Emily."

And then their lips would meet — a forbidden collision of longing and need. Emily tasted like stardust, and Klaus lost himself in her. They explored each other — the curve of her spine, the freckles on her face — until the ship's artificial gravity threatened to tear them apart.

But Wei was always there, watching from the shadows. She cornered Klaus during meals, engaged him in technical debates, and invited him to her quarters. "We're explorers," she said. "We take risks."

And so, Klaus found himself torn between two women — the brilliant geologist who ignited his passion and the ambitious engineer who challenged his mind. Emily's laughter echoed in his dreams, but Wei's whispered promises haunted him.

"Klaus," Wei said, her voice low and seductive. "We're on the brink of discovery. Don't you want to unravel the mysteries of the universe together?"

He hesitated, torn between ambition and desire. But when Emily kissed him beneath the stars, he knew — he was lost. Love had defied gravity, and they were caught in its pull.

And so, in those forbidden moments, their hearts became celestial bodies — colliding, burning, and leaving trails of light across the vastness of space.

The Martian Ball

The ballroom was a makeshift affair — a fusion of Earth elegance and Martian minimalism. The crew had transformed the cargo hold into a glittering space, complete with shimmering fabric and holographic stars. Emily wore a crimson dress that clung to her curves, and Klaus borrowed a suit that made him look more dashing than any scientist had a right to be.

Wei glided in, her eyes fixed on Klaus. Her gown was midnight blue, and her hair was swept up in an intricate bun. She moved with grace, her steps calculated. "May the best scientist win," she said, her smile too sweet.

Emily's heart raced. She'd danced with Klaus in the observation deck, but this was different — a public declaration of desire. As the music swirled around them, she took Klaus's hand, and they stepped onto the holographic dance floor.

"You're a brilliant scientist," Wei murmured, cutting in. "But love requires strategy."

Emily's grip on Klaus tightened. She'd studied Martian geology, but this was a different kind of terrain — a battlefield of hearts. Klaus hesitated, torn between ambition and longing. His analytical mind calculated the risks, but his heart yearned for something more.

The dance was a collision of desire and rivalry. Emily's crimson dress brushed against Klaus's suit, and Wei's midnight blue gown spun in elegant circles. The crew watched — their fellow astronauts, Commander Harris, even the ship's AI, all curious spectators in this cosmic drama.

"Choose," Emily whispered to Klaus. "Choose the stars or the equations. Choose me."

Wei's eyes bore into him. "We're explorers," she said. "We take risks. And love is the greatest risk of all."

And then Klaus did something unexpected. He pulled both women into his arms — a celestial embrace. "Perhaps," he said, "we can explore love together."

And so, beneath the holographic constellations, they danced — a trio of hearts entangled in the gravity of their desires ended up in a ménage à trois. The stars watched, its ancient secrets whispering through the walls. Love defied logic, and in that moment, they were more than astronauts — they were cosmic adventurers.

Celestial Rivalry

The Ares Horizon's engines hummed with tension. Emily and Wei had once shared whispered secrets and stolen kisses, but now their relationship had shifted. They were no longer lovers; they were rivals.

Klaus was the fulcrum, and he was the cause of their celestial discord. His analytical mind had dissected scientific mysteries, but it was his presence that ignited the rivalry. Emily watched him from across the lab, her red hair pulled back in frustration. Klaus was engrossed in his research, careless and oblivious to the cosmic collision brewing around him.

Wei, petite and determined, approached Klaus during a break. "Professor Müller," she said, her voice sweet as Martian honey, "have you considered the implications of the pyramid's function?"

Klaus glanced up, his blue eyes narrowing. "I've been analyzing the data," he replied. "But I don't need distractions."

Emily, unable to resist, joined the conversation. "Distractions like our shared memories?" she quipped.

Wei's cheeks flushed, and Klaus's jaw tightened. "We're professionals," he said. "Our mission is —"

"— to unravel Martian secrets," Emily finished. "But what about the secrets between us?"

Stellar Showdown

The rivalry escalated. Emily and Wei competed for Klaus's attention — subtle glances, intellectual debates, and late-night discussions about extraterrestrial artifacts. Klaus, torn between duty and desire, found himself drawn to both women.

One evening, Emily cornered Klaus in the observation deck. "You're avoiding us," she said. "Why?"

Klaus hesitated. "This mission — "

"— more than science," Emily interrupted. "We're echoes of Mars, remember? Our hearts pulse with the same curiosity that drove ancient civilizations."

Wei, eavesdropping from the shadows, stepped forward. "Klaus," she said, her voice trembling, "who do you choose?"

He studied their faces — the fiery geologist and the enigmatic engineer. "I choose knowledge," he said finally. "The molecule structure in this probe — they hold the key."

Emily's heart shattered. She retreated to her quarters, tears blurring her vision. Wei followed, her tiny frame filled with determination. "We can't let him destroy us," she whispered.

Emily wiped her tears. "We're explorers," she said. "But we're also human."

Together, they devised a plan. As Klaus worked late one night, making chemical analyses, they confronted him. "Choose," Emily demanded. "Us or your experiments."

Klaus hesitated, torn between love and duty. "I —" he began.

But Wei stepped forward, her eyes fierce. "We choose ourselves," she said. "Our hearts, our desires."

And so, they sabotaged the chemical experiment — a cosmic betrayal. Klaus watched in horror as the dissolution of his probe. He was at a loss for words, which was uncommon for him, who was so erudite and eloquent. He was completely shocked. After a few moments he shaked his head in resignation and said: "Do you know what you just did?"

As the spacecraft hurtled further toward Mars, the tension remained. Emily and Wei sat together, their fingers entwined. Klaus, once their center, was now an echo — a distant star fading into the cosmic background.

"We did what we had to," Wei said softly.

Emily nodded. "But at what cost?"

And so, the celestial rivalry left scars — their love fractured, their hearts echoing with regret.

And thus, the three astronauts approached to Mars, their cosmic dance forever altered.

The "Celestial Rivalry" between the two women would be a cautionary tale — a reminder that even among the stars, love could burn as brightly as it consumed.

Chapter 5: Descent

Approach to Mars

As Mars loomed larger in the viewport, the crew's excitement intensified. They huddled around the control panels, practicing landing simulations. The Martian soil — red and mysterious — was no longer an abstract concept; it was the ground they would soon touch.

There it is!

Mars, the fourth planet from the Sun, is accompanied in its celestial journey by two small and intriguing moons: Phobos and Deimos. These moons, named after the Greek gods of fear and terror, respectively, are starkly different from Earth's Moon and offer unique insights into the mysteries of our solar system.

Phobos is the larger Moon, whereas Deimos is smaller, more distant and less affected by Mars' gravitational forces, resulting in a more stable orbit. Unlike Phobos, Deimos has a smoother, less cratered surface, likely due to a layer of regolith, or loose debris, that blankets the moon. Its largest craters are significantly smaller than those on Phobos, and the overall appearance is more subdued, with fewer prominent features.

Navigating the Martian Gravitational Field

As The Ares Horizon nears Mars, it transitions from a steady cruise through the vacuum of space to an intricate dance with the planet's gravity. The approach is meticulously calculated, requiring precise adjustments to The Ares Horizon's trajectory to ensure it enters the Martian gravitational field at the correct angle and speed. The slightest miscalculation can mean the difference between a successful orbit insertion and a catastrophic failure.

Orbital Insertion: The Critical Maneuver

The most critical phase of entering Mars orbit is the orbital insertion maneuver. This involves firing The Ares Horizon's main engine to slow it down sufficiently to be captured by Mars' gravity. This burn, often lasting several minutes, is conducted with a precision akin to threading a needle from millions of miles away. During this time, communication with Earth is typically limited due to the time it takes for signals to travel across vast distances, adding an element of suspense and tension.

Visual and Sensory Experience: The Martian Encounter

For the entire crew experiencing this event, the visual and sensory experience is breathtaking. From space, Mars looms large, a rust-colored orb with distinct surface features such as the massive Olympus Mons volcano, the vast Valles Marineris canyon, and the polar ice caps. As The Ares Horizon draws closer, these features become more defined, offering a view unlike any other.

Inside The Ares Horizon, the crew felt the subtle vibrations and hear the hum of the engines as they execute the burn. The cabin's displays showed real-time data, providing a constant stream of information about the spacecraft's position, velocity, and trajectory.

Entering the orbit of Mars is a monumental achievement that epitomizes the pinnacle of human engineering, scientific curiosity, and the relentless quest to explore the unknown. This process, while deeply rooted in complex physics and precise calculations, is also a journey marked by awe, anticipation, and the profound realization of humanity's place in the cosmos.

Sophie, her blond hair floating in microgravity, leaned over to Ivan. "Ivan," she whispered, "will you play your guitar for the Martians?"

He grinned, adjusting the strap of his acoustic guitar. "Perhaps," he replied. "But who's to say they won't have their own music? Maybe they'll teach us a tune we've never heard."

The crew prepared to transfer to the Mars Lander.

Touchdown

During its descent, the Mars lander encountered several challenges as it made its way to the Martian surface.

During the first 25 seconds of parachute descent, the lander jettisoned its heat shield. The heat shield protected the lander during atmospheric entry, but it needed to be discarded to allow the lander's instruments to operate effectively. About two minutes after the parachute opened and one minute before landing.

The lander extended its three legs. These legs provided stability and ensured a safe touchdown on the Martian surface.

As the spacecraft descended, it used radar to sense its velocity and measure the distance to the ground. This real-time data allowed the Mars lander to adjust its descent trajectory and ensure a precise landing.

The lander had to avoid potential hazards such as large rocks, craters, or uneven terrain. The onboard sensors and algorithms helped it make real-time decisions to steer clear of any dangerous obstacles.

Mars' thin atmosphere posed challenges during descent. The lander had to rely on its parachute and retrorockets to slow down effectively without burning up or crashing.

The lander communicated with Earth through the relay satellites in Mars orbit. However, the communication delay (due to the vast distance) meant that the lander had to execute its descent autonomously based on pre-programmed instructions. The average one-way communication delay is about 12.5 minutes, given the average distance of 225 million kilometers.

The Martian surface stretched out before them, a barren expanse of rust-colored sand and jagged rocks. Commander Harris squinted through the viewport of the lander, his heart pounding with anticipation. He was leading an elite team of astronauts on the most important mission in human history: the exploration of an ancient Martian pyramid. This was Mars — the planet that had haunted humanity's dreams for centuries.

The Martian lander shuddered as it pierced the thin atmosphere, flames licking its heat shield. Commander Harris gripped the control yoke, his knuckles white. The descent was always the most perilous part of any mission, but this was different. He'd flown combat missions in Earth's skies, but this was different. Mars was unforgiving— a desolate beauty that hid its secrets well.

Beside him, Emily adjusted her red hairband, her brilliant green eyes scanning the horizon. As the team's geologist, she was eager to uncover the secrets hidden beneath the Martian soil. She had studied every pixel of Martian terrain from orbit. Now, she was about to touch down on its surface.

"Steady, Commander," Emily's voice crackled over the intercom. "We're entering the final phase." Her red hair was pulled back in a tight bun, and her green eyes sparkled with determination.

Commander Harris adjusted the thrusters, guiding the Mars lander toward the designated landing site — the Bamberg Crater, which is a significant geographical landmark in the Cydonia Mensae region. The Bamberg Crater is near an ancient canyon system. The specific canyon system within Cydonia Mensae does not have a well-known, individual name like larger Martian features such as Valles Marineris at the equator of Mars. The valleys and canyons in this region are generally referred to collectively as part of the Cydonia Mensae terrain.

Ivan adjusted his helmet. Then he cracked his knuckles and flexed his strong arms. His athletic frame strained against the restraints. His medical expertise would be crucial in this harsh environment. "We're almost there," he said, his accent thick. "Remember the training."

Wei checked her instruments, her petite frame belying the strength that lay within. "All systems are go," she confirmed, her eyes meeting those of Klaus, who nodded back with a calm assurance.

"Touchdown in T-minus 60 seconds," announced Ivan, his voice steady despite the palpable tension that filled the cabin.

Sophie leaned forward in her seat. "This is it," she whispered. "The moment we've all been waiting for."

Beside her, Wei muttered a prayer in Mandarin. She tapped her fingers nervously on the console. She had spent countless hours deciphering the ancient Martian hieroglyphs that adorned the pyramid they were about to explore. The symbols held the promise of answers - answers that could reshape human history.

The lander's thrusters fired, kicking up a cloud of red dust. The surface rushed toward them — a mosaic of craters and ancient riverbeds.

If the craters had their origin of a meteor hit or of a volcano, as they have learned with Emily's lecture, could not be made out at this speed. Commander Harris's heart pounded as he guided the lander toward a flat expanse.

The sun hung low, casting elongated shadows across the barren landscape. The shuttle's landing gear extended, and the Martian dust swirled as they touched down.

As the dust settled, the team unstrapped themselves and stood. The airlock hissed open, and they stepped onto Martian soil. The sky above was a pale pink, the sun a distant orange disk. They were on the cusp of making history.

The silence that followed was profound.

Commander Harris was the first to step out, his boots sinking into the reddish soil. The others followed suit, their helmets reflecting the alien world around them.

Ivan stepped out, scanning the horizon. The panorama left him speechless.

Wei adjusted her translator headset. She was sheer to busy to enjoy the scenery at the moment. She definitely wanted to fulfill her mission and not to forget anything.

Sophie held her breath. She felt excitement, but also fear of the unknown to come at the same time.

Unlike Sophie, Klaus remained cool and ready to go for the task without any hesitation. He clutched his data pad.

"Welcome to Mars," Commander Harris said, his voice echoing inside his helmet.

Emily, the First Officer, joined Commander Harris at the hatch outside. "We made it," she said. "We are the only humans on Mars now."

Now Ivan, the Second Officer, joined them and said euphorically: "Let's find out what secrets this planet holds."

Commander Harris nodded. "But what awaits us here? What did the ancient Martians leave behind?"

They had their orders — to explore, collect samples, and search for signs of past life. But Commander Harris sensed there was more — an undercurrent of destiny pulling them toward the Martian secrets.

On the edge of the Bamberg crater, the astronauts had a breathtaking view of the system of valleys and gorges. This bizarre landscape will now be their new home for the next few months.

As the dust that had been stirred up by the landing continued to settle, Wei pointed to the distant horizon. "Commander, look!"

Commander Harris squinted. There, half-buried in the sand, stood a five-sided pyramid.

And so, with hearts full of anticipation, they set off toward the distant pyramid — a relic of an ancient civilization that had vanished eons ago. The Martian winds whispered their secrets, and the astronauts pressed forward, ready to unravel the mysteries of the red planet.

The crew was well aware that this would be a journey to test their resolve, challenge their beliefs, and reveal the echoes of a civilization lost to time.

Chapter 6: The New Home

The Pyramid of Needs

It was a tiresome walk for the six astronauts, but they have trained for this on Earth before for months together.

However, the gravity on Mars, being roughly one third of that on Earth, offers both advantages and challenges for human physical performance and stamina. While reduced weight makes movement and certain physical tasks easier, the long-term health implications, including muscle atrophy, bone density loss, and cardiovascular deconditioning, pose significant challenges.

Human bodies are highly adaptable, and with time, individuals living on Mars may acclimate to the lower gravity. Exercise routines designed to mimic the effects of Earth's gravity, such as resistance training and the use of specially designed exercise equipment, have been regularly performed by all crew members during space flight to help maintain muscle and bone health. Rehabilitation protocols for returning to Earth after extended periods on Mars have been established and a compulsory, as the body would need to readjust to Earth's stronger gravitational pull.

It seemed to take an endless amount of time before they approached their actual destination or "region of interest", as Emily had called it in her lecture previously: the volcano with the adjacent pyramid.

Slowly but surely on the horizon, they could make out their habitat and the Mars Return Vehicle (MRV), which was to take them back into orbit to The Ares Horizon. These things had already been transported there before their manned mission several years ago.

With habitat, it was vital that the life support systems worked and that the supplies were delivered undamaged by the unmanned probes. Otherwise they would starve and die of thirst.

The MRV's systems must also function reliably, otherwise they would be trapped here on the planet. The power would be delivered through solar panels with battery backup that should be not broken or covered by dust. Moreover the MRV (usual crew capacity of 4-6 astronauts) must provide a 48-hour life support system for ascent and orbit rendezvous.

Producing fuel on Mars for the MRV works through the Sabatier reaction and solid oxide electrolysis. These processes leverage the abundant CO_2 in the Martian atmosphere and water resources to produce methane and oxygen, providing a sustainable solution for return missions to Earth and supporting longer-term human presence on Mars.

However, the technology must function perfectly despite adverse conditions such as sandstorms and exposure to intense UV radiation on a planet without an atmosphere worth mentioning as a protective shield.

Martian sandstorms are a notable feature of the planet's weather, occurring regularly and sometimes on a global scale. While the planet's thin atmosphere limits the force of the winds compared to Earth, the fine dust particles and atmospheric conditions allow for significant and frequent dust storm activity.

Speak of the devil, a storm was approaching…

Commander Harris was the first to make it to the habitat followed by the engineers backing him: Emily and Wei.

In concert, the engineers gave literally a red light before booting up the systems and emitted in an unmistakable sound:"Stop!"

Emily said:"First we have to make the primary system test run. When everything works out fine, then we will give the go!"

After running the first test run, they held the thumbs up and said in chorus:"Check!" and "Go!"

The airlock released its passengers into a breathable atmosphere at room temperature. The average outside temperature on Mars is approximately -63°C (-81°F).

Before they took off their helmets, Ivan unexpectedly held Sophie from behind and shouted:"Stop, Sophie!" She was scared and screamed. "What about the alien monster over there?"

When Sophie saw that he had made fun of her, she angrily pushed him aside.

Commander Harris frowned and took of is helmet. "Alright, you lovebirds. Now stop playing kindergarten games, we have a serious mission to attend to."

Because of the upcoming storm, they decided not to check the MRV yet, but rather sitting duck in their habitat. Fortunately, all the food parcels had arrived undamaged.

In this way, the basic needs of the famous Maslow's hierarchy of needs, often depicted as a pyramid, were secured: they had a shelter with beds to sleep, air to breath, food and water. And all of them were well and sound without injuries.

Everything beyond that was pure luxury at the moment.

Solving a Dilemma Sitation

The Martian habitat hummed with life support systems, but it wasn't immune to glitches. The crew members were first relieved that the primary systems seemed to worked properly. However, one fateful night, the habitat's automated systems malfunctioned. Lights flickered, and the temperature dropped precipitously. The cause has been found quickly by the team's engineers Emily and Wei: one of the habitat's heating units malfunctioned due to a faulty sensor in a bunk bed compartment. The temperature plummeted rapidly, threatening the crew's well-being. The engineers scrambled to find the issue, but the repair would take hours. Meanwhile, frost formed on the walls, and the crew's breath hung in the air like ghostly wisps. Therefore, they needed to isolate and shut down this faulty bunk bed compartment.

Commander Harris said: "Now we have to solve the follwing dilemma situation: we are six astronauts, but only five beds available. Who will draw the short straw?"

Suprisingly, Emily suggested:"I will sacrifice myself, I will sleep with Wei." Wei was hissing in anger.

Klaus laughed loud and said:"Wei, this was irony and was Emily's British sense of humor."

Emily was pleased to see that Klaus understood her humor and winked at Klaus. She still has not forgiven his rejection of love after the "Celestial Rivalry", although she secretly had hopes again.

Commander Harris took the floor:"So we must establish a rotation system where each person takes turns sleeping on a bed."

Sophie shivered, wrapping herself in a thermal blanket. "Ivan, the heating unit is down. It's freezing in here."

Ivan, equally chilled, nodded."We need to conserve body heat. A shared bunk bed is our best option."

Sophie stepped forward and said:"Not at all. As you all know, Ivan and I are together, so we will be in the bed together. Problem has been solved."

Ivan nodded and said willingly:" What you do for the country and the mission..."

They climbed into the narrow bunk, their breath visible in the frigid air. Sophie's blond hair spilled across the pillow, and Ivan's brown eyes held a mix of concern and determination.

"Teamwork, right?" Sophie said, her teeth chattering.

"Absolutely," Ivan replied. "We'll survive this together."

As they huddled close, sharing warmth and whispered stories, Sophie realized that sometimes adversity forged the strongest bonds. The malfunctioning habitat had brought them closer — literally and metaphorically.

And so, beneath the Martian sky, Sophie and Ivan found solace in their shared bunk, their hearts thawing even as the temperature plummeted.

Sophie and Ivan found themselves sharing a bunk bed while their fellow astronauts retained their individual berths.

The Tempest

The Martian sky had been deceptively calm — a pale blue expanse stretching infinitely. But on the third day, as the crew ventured farther from their habitat into the Martian pyramid's direction, the horizon darkened again. Emily noticed it first — a distant wall of dust rising like a spectral beast.

"Storm incoming," she warned, her voice crackling over the radio. The astronauts scrambled back, seeking shelter. Commander Harris's heart raced. They had trained for this, but simulations couldn't capture the raw fury of a Martian tempest.

The wind howled, whipping fine particles against their visors. Visibility dropped to mere meters. Klaus stumbled, his suit sensors detecting pressure changes. "Hold on!" he shouted, gripping a rock.

The storm swallowed them whole. Emily's geology tools vanished in the maelstrom. Emily clung to the tether connecting her to the habitat. Wei's engineering mind calculated the strain on their suits.

And Sophie — she sang. Her voice cut through the chaos, a fragile melody against the raging elements. "We're still here," she sang, "defying Mars' wrath."

Hours blurred into eternity. The storm battered their habitat, its metal groaning. Ivan's guitar lay abandoned, buried under red drifts. But they held on, six souls clinging to life, to purpose.

When the tempest finally subsided, they emerged. The landscape had changed — the riverbed erased, rocks rearranged. Emily's eyes widened. "Look!" she said, pointing. A fissure had opened, revealing layers of Martian history — a geological diary etched by wind and time.

They stood on the brink of revelation, battered but unbroken. Mars had tested them, and they had survived. As the dust settled, Commander Harris whispered, "We're still pioneers."

And the red planet whispered back, secrets swirling in its thin air.

Chapter 7: The Martian Pyramid

The Martian dawn cast a ruddy glow over the ancient pyramid, its five sides rising majestically from the desert floor. The structure, partially buried in dust and time, loomed over the astronauts, a silent testament to a forgotten civilization? The team, now fully acclimated to their surroundings, prepared for their first thorough exploration of the enigmatic edifice.

Commander Harris stood at the pyramid's base, his imposing figure silhouetted against the rising sun. "Alright, team. Let's make history."

The Exterior: Awe-Inspiring Architecture

The pyramid, towering nearly 60 meters (200 feet) high, was constructed from enormous blocks of an unfamiliar, glassy black stone. These blocks, fitted together with such precision that not even a Martian dust particle could slip through, gave the structure a seamless appearance. Each of the five sides of the pyramid was adorned with intricate carvings and hieroglyphs, their meaning lost to time but their craftsmanship evident in every detail.

Emily, her geological instruments ready, approached the pyramid with a mixture of reverence and excitement. "The stone used here is unlike anything I've seen. It's not native to Mars."

Klaus, intrigued, crouched beside her to examine the rock. "It's almost as if it was imported, which implies an advanced level of technology. Fascinating."

The pyramid's surface, though worn by millennia of exposure to harsh Martian elements, still retained a polished sheen. The smooth, almost reflective surface caught the light in a way that made the entire structure seem to glow from within. Along the base, the stone was covered in a fine layer of Martian dust, which the team carefully brushed away to reveal more of the detailed inscriptions.

The Symbols and Hieroglyphs

Wei, eager to prove herself, joined Emily and Klaus, her tiny frame dwarfed by the massive stones. "We need to document every detail. The hieroglyphs might give us clues about their civilization."

Emily and Wei exchanged a look, their earlier rivalry now blown away by their shared curiosity. They began methodically recording the inscriptions, their hands brushing occasionally as they worked side by side.

The hieroglyphs, etched deeply into the stone, depicted scenes of daily life, celestial maps, and intricate geometric patterns. Some of the symbols were familiar, resembling ancient Earth languages of Sumerian and ancient Egyptian origin, as Wei had presented in her lecture recently, while other inscriptions were entirely alien. These carvings told tales of a thriving Martian society, their remarkable achievements, and the enigmatic mysteries that defined their civilization.

Scenes of Daily Life

The lower sections of the pyramid were adorned with detailed depictions of daily life in ancient Mars. The carvings showed Martian beings, humanoid in shape but with distinctive elongated limbs and large, expressive eyes, engaged in various activities.

Agriculture and Harvesting:

The Martians were shown tending to vast fields of strange, tubular plants that grew in the arid Martian soil. They used advanced tools that emitted beams of light, which seemed to encourage the plants to grow. There were also scenes of harvest festivals, where the Martians celebrated the bounty of their land with music, dance, and communal feasts.

Emily, was the first to speak. "The carvings show a sophisticated understanding of their environment. The agricultural scenes, in particular, suggest they had mastered techniques for growing crops in the Martian soil. The tools they used emitted beams of light, possibly to stimulate plant growth. This implies they had advanced biotechnological knowledge."

Klaus nodded in agreement. "Indeed, Emily. The tubular plants depicted are unlike anything on Earth, but their cultivation methods indicate a high level of agronomy. If we can understand these techniques, it could revolutionize how we approach farming in extreme environments, even back on Earth."

Emily was still very focused on the research work, but at the same time she had to admit to herself that feelings of affection to Klaus surged again inside her.

Family and Social Structure:

Another set of carvings depicted Martian family units. Parents were shown teaching their offspring, who appeared to be smaller versions of themselves, about their culture and traditions. The emphasis on community and knowledge transfer suggested a society that valued education and social cohesion.

Ivan commented on these depictions of Martian families and social structures. "These carvings indicate a strong emphasis on community and education. Knowledge transfer was a cornerstone of their society, likely contributing to their advancements. Their medical practices, if any of the symbols relate to healthcare, could be far beyond what we currently understand."

Emily added, "The familial scenes also suggest that they valued social cohesion, which might have played a role in their ability to achieve such technological and cultural heights."

Technological and Architectural Marvels

Moving higher up the pyramid, the carvings shifted focus to the technological achievements of the Martians. These sections illustrated their advanced understanding of engineering and architecture.

Wei pointed to a section of carvings showing the Martians' cityscapes. "Their cities were masterpieces of engineering. The floating platforms and interconnecting bridges suggest they had developed anti-gravity technology or something similar. Look at the energy conduits — they harnessed power from the planet's core and solar energy with incredible efficiency."

Cityscapes and Structures:

The Martians lived in sprawling cities filled with towering structures made of the same glassy black stone as the pyramid. These buildings were interconnected by intricate networks of bridges and walkways. The carvings depicted bustling urban life, with Martians navigating their cities using both footpaths and floating platforms that hovered above the ground.

Energy and Power Sources:

Several panels illustrated the Martians harnessing energy from the planet's core and the sun. They used devices that appeared to be solar collectors and geothermal taps. One particularly detailed carving showed a large, central power hub surrounded by conduits that distributed energy to different parts of their city.

Celestial Exploration and Astronomy

The upper sections of the pyramid were dedicated to the Martians' fascination with the stars and their exploration of the cosmos.

Stellar Maps and Observatories:

Intricate maps of the night sky were etched into the stone, showcasing the Martians' knowledge of constellations, planets, and celestial events. They had built observatories, depicted as tall, slender towers with large, spherical tops, possibly housing advanced telescopes. These observatories were shown aligned with various celestial bodies, indicating the Martians' precise astronomical calculations.

Ivan leaned closer, his breath fogging the visor of his helmet. "These glyphs," he said, „they speak of cosmic alignment, of star maps etched into the very stones."

Wei adjusted her translator headset. "The Martians understood celestial navigation," she murmured.

Commander Harris studied the pyramid's base. "We're standing on the threshold of discovery," he said. "What lies within?"

Spacecraft and Interplanetary Travel:

A particularly fascinating series of carvings depicted the Martians' endeavors in space travel. They had constructed sleek, aerodynamic spacecraft capable of interplanetary voyages. These vessels were shown departing from large spaceports and traveling to other planets, suggesting that the Martians had explored their solar system extensively.

Sophie was fascinated by the illustrations of spacecraft. "And their space travel capabilities are astounding. These vessels — they're sleek, built for interplanetary travel. If we can decode how they powered these ships, it could push our own space exploration efforts forward by decades."

Ivan joined her and said in a charme:"Well, where would you like us to run away to together? To Andromeda galaxy?"

Sophie winked coyly: :"I don't care, as long as you don't leave me."

Ivan made the gesture of a kiss with his hand directed at her from his helmet.

Cultural and Spiritual Practices

The carvings also revealed the spiritual and cultural life of the Martians, hinting at their beliefs and rituals.

Temples and Ceremonies:

The Martians built grand temples, depicted with soaring arches and intricate mosaics. Inside these temples, they performed ceremonies that appeared to honor celestial events and natural phenomena. The carvings showed Martians in elaborate robes, gathered around altars and engaging in ritualistic dances and chants.

Hieroglyphs and Sacred Texts:

The hieroglyphs themselves were a testament to the Martians' written language and record-keeping. These symbols, which Emily and Wei painstakingly documented, conveyed complex ideas and narratives. Some panels seemed to function as sacred texts, recounting the creation myths and the Martians' understanding of the universe.

Mysteries and Enigmatic Symbols

The team then turned their attention to the more mysterious symbols — the gateways and the guardians.

Wei highlighted a section with the celestial maps. "These maps show a detailed understanding of the cosmos. Their observatories were aligned with celestial bodies, indicating precise astronomical calculations. This knowledge could have been crucial for navigation and perhaps even for using the gateway."

Commander Harris interjected, "The gateway is the most intriguing aspect. These carvings show Martians passing through it, suggesting it was a portal to other worlds or dimensions. If we can understand how to activate it, we might unlock the ability to travel vast distances instantaneously."

The Gateway:

Several carvings depicted a mysterious gateway, a large, circular structure adorned with glyphs and glowing with an inner light. Martians were shown passing through this gateway, suggesting it was a portal to other worlds or dimensions. The exact nature and function of this gateway remained a tantalizing mystery, sparking endless speculation among the team.

The Guardians:

Another recurring motif was the presence of guardian figures. These guardians, always depicted in pairs, stood watch over important sites and relics. They seemed to possess a protective function, perhaps safeguarding the knowledge and treasures of the Martian civilization.

Klaus, looking at the guardian figures, expressed his thoughts. "These guardians — always depicted in pairs — suggest they played a significant role in protecting important sites and relics. They might have been more than just symbolic; perhaps they were part of an advanced security system."

The Great Cataclysm – the Catastrophe:

Towards the top of the pyramid, the carvings took a darker turn, depicting scenes of turmoil and destruction. These panels showed a great cataclysm that befell the Martians, with cities crumbling and the ground splitting open. The carvings suggested that this event led to the decline of their civilization, but the cause remained unclear, shrouded in layers of symbolism and cryptic hieroglyphs.

The discussion took a somber turn as they examined the scenes depicting the great cataclysm.

Emily spoke softly, "These carvings of destruction show cities crumbling and the ground splitting open. The Martians faced a catastrophic event, but the cause remains unclear. It could have been natural, like a massive tectonic shift, or something else entirely."

Ivan added, "Understanding this cataclysm is crucial. If it was a Martian-made disaster, we need to learn from their mistakes to avoid a similar fate for our own civilizations."

Drawing Conclusions

After a tiresome sol (a Martian day is approximately 24 hours, 39 minutes, and thus a slightly longer than an Earth day), the crew returned to the habitat exhausted. However, everybody was still on adrenaline due to the exciting discoveries.

When they have settled after the joint dinner, Commander Harris summarized their findings:"We've uncovered a wealth of information about a sophisticated and advanced Martian society. Their achievements in agriculture, technology, and space travel are extraordinary. What mesmerized me a lot was at the peak of their advanced civilization they obviously encountered the events of a downfall of unknown origin. Our next steps should focus on finding a way inside the pyramid."

Sophie nodded, her eyes bright with determination. "We're on the brink of something monumental. Let's make sure we honor their legacy by learning all we can and applying it wisely." Ivan pressed her hand in support.

Emily and Wei shared a determined look. "Agreed," Emily said. "And we think, we found a hint to get in, but it needs a lot of digging." Klaus made a secret link to Emily and both of them knew that they could not act out upcoming feelings in front of the others, in particular Wei, as long as they are caved in here.

So shortly after the sol's evening session they all went to sleep. They climbed into their seperated compartments, while Sophie and Ivan lay entwined in their shared berth.

Well, not everybody was falling asleep. Emily was still moved about the emotions that had come up again and was permanently thinkuing of Klaus. How did this happen to her again? She could not give a reasonable explanation.

Chapter 8: The Alien Stone Face

On next sol, in renewed focus and a sense of unity, the team set to work, driven by the knowledge that their discoveries on Mars could reshape humanity's understanding of the universe and its place within it. Emily and Wei with their joined understanding in engineering, Earth ancient history architecture made out the most probable side to find an entrance gate.

Ivan and Sophie, meanwhile, circled the structure, searching for the entrance way accordingly. Their budding romance lent a lightness to their steps, a sense of adventure.

"Here," Sophie called, pointing to a section where the sand seemed disturbed. "This might be a way in."

After several hours, they cleared away more of the sand with the help of machines, a colossal stone face emerged.

Shortly afterwards, Ivan uncovered a hidden entrance: "Looks like we've found the entrance."

The stone face carved into the front of the pyramid seemed to follow them with its eyes.

Sophie whispered: "That's incredible. It must be some kind of guardian. Or a warning."

Ivan nodded, awe in his voice. "Or a marker, indicating something significant behind it."

They called the other crew members for help.

Wei held out her gloved hand. "He's sentient," she said, "a consciousness trapped in stone."

Emily said: "The pyramid seems to be a cosmic library. A repository of knowledge left behind by a starfaring race."

Commander Harris nodded. "And we're the custodians," he said. "The ones chosen to unlock its secrets."

The face was both alien and eerily human, with large, almond-shaped eyes, a pronounced brow, and an expression of serene wisdom. Its mouth was slightly open, as if about to speak, and intricate patterns adorned its forehead and cheeks.

The stone face stood nearly 20 meters (65 feet) tall, an imposing and awe-inspiring figure guarding the entrance to the pyramid. The face was carved from the same glassy black stone that made up the rest of the pyramid, yet it seemed to possess a unique quality, as though imbued with a consciousness that had watched over the Martian landscape for millennia.

The Eyes

The eyes were the most striking feature of the face. They were large and almond-shaped, with a slight upward slant at the outer edges, giving them a contemplative and wise appearance. Despite being carved from stone, the eyes seemed almost alive, as if they could see through time and space. The pupils were inset with a different type of stone, possibly an ancient form of onyx or obsidian, which caught the light and made the eyes glimmer eerily in the Martian dawn.

Around the eyes, complex patterns were etched into the stone, resembling a blend of celestial maps and mathematical designs. These patterns might have represented the civilization's understanding of the cosmos or their spiritual beliefs.

The Brow and Forehead

The brow was pronounced and powerful, giving the face an air of authority and intelligence. The forehead was wide and adorned with intricate carvings that flowed seamlessly into the patterns around the eyes. At the center of the forehead, just above the brow, was a large, circular emblem that looked like a third eye. This emblem was surrounded by radiating lines and geometric shapes, suggesting it held significant meaning, perhaps symbolizing enlightenment or a higher state of consciousness.

The Cheeks and Nose

The cheeks were smooth and gently curved, contrasting with the more angular features of the brow and eyes. They bore delicate carvings of what appeared to be flowing lines, like the tendrils of an alien plant or the currents of a Martian river. These lines converged at the nose, which was long and straight, with flared nostrils that gave the face a sense of dignity and strength.

The Mouth

The mouth was slightly open, revealing a mechanism inside that appeared to be a locking system for the hidden entrance. The lips were full and well-defined, carved with such skill that they seemed capable of speech. Inside the mouth, the team could see interlocking gears and levers, hinting at the advanced technology that lay hidden behind the stone façade.

The Jawline and Chin

The jawline was strong and angular, leading down to a broad, square chin. The chin itself was adorned with additional carvings, including more symbols and what looked like depictions of ancient Martian creatures. These carvings flowed seamlessly into the base of the face, connecting it to the pyramid as if the entire structure was a single, unified piece of art.

The Overall Impression

The stone face exuded a sense of timeless wisdom and authority, as if it were the guardian of all the secrets contained within the pyramid. Its expression was one of serene contemplation, and despite its alien features, there was a strange familiarity to it, as though it bridged the gap between human and Martian civilization.

The Carvings and Symbolism

The intricate patterns and carvings that adorned the face were not merely decorative but seemed to hold deep symbolic meaning. The celestial maps suggested an advanced understanding of astronomy, possibly indicating that the civilization that built the pyramid had mapped the stars and perhaps even traveled among them. The mathematical designs hinted at a highly developed scientific knowledge, and the flowing lines and geometric shapes suggested a culture that valued both art and science.

Discovering the Entrance

Commander Harris gathered the team. "Let's figure out how to get inside."

Emily knelt to examine the sandstone blocks. "I am working on it. The pyramid is a gateway," she said. "A portal to knowledge beyond our wildest dreams."

Sophie shivered. "And dangers," she added. "The Martians guarded their secrets."

Klaus scanned the horizon. "We're not alone," he said. Look — there, in the distance.

A shadow moved — a figure emerging from the Martian dust. It was Ivan's turn to shiver. "An apparition?" he wondered aloud.

Klaus turned and retorted: "This must have been a Fata Morgana."

Sophie agreed and said:"Yes, this was merely a mirage." That was what she officially said, but she was thinking otherwise, hoping that they really have been optically deceived.

On the one hand, after decades of unmanned Mars exploration, there had definitely been no evidence of existing life. On the other hand, inspite of extense research, the discovery of a Martian pyramid has slipped through up until now. How could this have happened so easily? Or were there people in power who wanted to prevent certain discoveries from reaching the public? But that would already be enough in the realm of conspiracy theories. Therefore, Sophie quickly dismissed these thoughts, joined the group and concentrated on their current problem, how to open the entrance.

Emily, studying the face, noticed something peculiar. "Look at the mouth. It's slightly open, and there's a mechanism inside."

Wei, with her engineering background, stepped forward. "It looks like a locking mechanism. If we can figure out how to activate it, we might be able to open the door."

They examined the stone face closely, noting that the mouth's opening revealed a series of small, interlocking gears and levers. Above the face, embedded in the stone, was a series of symbols arranged in a circular pattern.

Emily, tracing the symbols with her fingers, suddenly had an idea. "These symbols match some of the hieroglyphs we documented earlier. Maybe it's a code."

Working together, the team deciphered the symbols, discovering that they represented numbers and directions. With Wei's expertise, they aligned the gears and levers according to the pattern.

As they completed the sequence, a low rumble echoed through the pyramid. The stone face's mouth opened wider, revealing a hidden panel with a large, circular handle.

Commander Harris took a deep breath and grasped the handle. "Here goes nothing."

He turned the handle, and with a loud, ancient groan, the massive stone slab slowly slid aside, revealing a dark passageway beyond.

Chapter 9: The Cosmic Library

The Passageway

As the stone slab slid open with a deep, resonant groan, the entrance to the pyramid revealed a dark passageway that beckoned the astronauts into the ancient Martian structure.

Commander Harris gathered the team. "Let's move in together. Stay alert and document everything."

Switching on their headlamps, the team stepped cautiously into the unknown, their lights cutting through the thick darkness and casting eerie shadows on the walls.

The air composition on Mars is quite different from that of Earth. The Martian atmosphere is thin and composed primarily of carbon dioxide. Therefore, Martian environment posed its own set of challenges. The team wore specially designed suits to protect them from the thin atmosphere and extreme temperatures. The suits, equipped with advanced filtration systems, allowed them to breathe comfortably while also keeping out the pervasive Martian dust.

The walls, made of the same glassy black material as the exterior, shimmered slightly under their lights, reflecting faint hues of blue and green.

Emily ran her fingers along the wall's surface. "This material... it's not just stone. There's a crystalline structure embedded within. It's like nothing I've ever seen."

Wei knelt to examine the floor. "These grooves... they're not random. This was deliberately designed to channel something — maybe water, or some form of energy."

As they advanced, the walls of the passageway became more intricately decorated. Carvings similar to those on the outside adorned the stone, but these were even more detailed, depicting scenes of Martian life in vivid relief.

The carvings along the passageway told a chronological story of the Martian civilization. The initial sections showed the early days, with Martians developing their technology and mastering their environment. The figures were shown building structures, experimenting with early energy sources, and mapping the stars.

Further along, the carvings transitioned to scenes of technological marvels. There were depictions of flying machines, vast underground cities, and complex energy grids. The Martians appeared to have achieved a high level of technological prowess, seamlessly integrating their advancements into everyday life.

Interspersed among the technological scenes were depictions of cultural and spiritual activities. Martians were shown participating in elaborate ceremonies, dancing around large stone altars, and engaging in what appeared to be communal meditation. These scenes suggested a deeply spiritual culture that revered both their technological achievements and the natural world.

As the team moved deeper into the passageway, they noticed faint, glowing lines along the walls and ceiling. These lines, barely perceptible at first, became more prominent as they progressed, casting a soft, ambient light that illuminated their path.

Sophie reached out to touch one of the glowing lines. "It feels warm. This must be some kind of ancient power source, still active after all these years."

Ivan examined the glowing lines with fascination. "This level of sustained energy production is extraordinary. They must have had a way to harness and store energy with incredible efficiency."

The Pyramid Chamber

After what felt like an eternity of walking through the winding passageway, the team emerged into a vast chamber. This room was enormous, with high ceilings and walls covered in more detailed carvings and hieroglyphs. At the center of the chamber stood a large, circular platform surrounded by stone plinths.

Emily was amazed:"This is incredible. These carvings depict their daily life, their rituals."

Klaus moved closer to a particularly detailed panel. "Look at this. It's a depiction of the gateway. They must have used it frequently."

Wei's eyes widened as she translated the symbols. "It says here that the gateway was a bridge between worlds, used by their scholars and explorers."

Commander Harris, standing at the center of the chamber, felt a chill run down his spine. "We need to find out how it works. This could be the key to understanding their entire civilization." Then he stepped onto the platform. "This must be a central hub of some sort. Look at these plinths — they're arranged in a deliberate pattern."

Emily, examining one of the plinths, found what appeared to be an ancient Martian text inscribed on its surface. "These symbols are different from the ones outside. They're more complex, almost like an advanced form of their written language."

Wei, scanning the platform, noticed a series of small, recessed circles. "These could be activation points. If we can figure out the sequence, we might be able to access whatever this chamber was designed to store."

Working together, the team carefully pressed the recessed circles in various combinations. After several attempts, a low hum filled the chamber, and the plinths began to glow with a soft blue light.

Holographic images flickered to life above each plinth, displaying detailed maps, diagrams, and streams of text in the Martian language.

Sophie's eyes widened. "This is their information library. We're looking at their history, their technology, everything."

Ivan, moving from one plinth to another, was captivated by a series of holographic images showing medical procedures and anatomical studies. "Their medical knowledge... it's incredibly advanced. We have so much to learn from them."

The team spent hours interacting with the holographic displays, each astronaut diving deep into their area of expertise. They took meticulous notes, recorded holograms, and translated texts, piecing together the Martian civilization's grand narrative.

Emily, engrossed in the geological data, commented:"Their understanding of planetary science was incredible. They managed to stabilize their environment and create sustainable ecosystems even in such harsh conditions."

Wei, analyzing the energy systems, added:"If we can replicate their energy technology, we could solve many of Earth's energy problems. Their efficiency and sustainability are beyond anything we have."

Ivan, still marveling at the medical holograms, said, "Their medical advancements could revolutionize our healthcare. Imagine curing diseases at a cellular level, regenerating damaged tissues instantly."

Commander Harris kept an eye on the time. "We need to prioritize what we can take back with us. Focus on the most critical information — energy, medical advancements, and the gateway mechanism."

As they delved deeper, the team discovered a series of encrypted holographic messages on the plinth dedicated to the gateway. These messages were from the last days of the Martian civilization, detailing their efforts to preserve their knowledge and ensure it could be accessed by future explorers.

Sophie, working with Emily and Wei, deciphered the final message. "They knew their end was coming. They encoded their knowledge to protect it from being lost. This gateway — it wasn't just a technological marvel; it was their last hope, a way to reach out to other civilizations and ensure their legacy endured."

Klaus reflecting on the biological data, added: "Their understanding of life itself was profound. They saw biology and technology as intertwined, using both to achieve a harmony we can only dream of."

Emily and Wei worked on translating the texts. "This will take time," Emily said, "but these documents could hold the key to understanding their technology and perhaps even the gateway."

Commander Harris ordered:"Dismissed! I can understand your enthusiasm, but that is enough for today. It is late already. We have to do a lot of homework now. We will return to this library tomorrow."

Emily and Wei reluctantly gave in and stood up to make their way back. They put Klaus in the middle and Sophie and Ivan followed as the rearguard.

As soon as they left the room, the holographic projection of the information library switched off automatically.

They had gathered enormous amounts of data today, which they used for the next uplink with Earth mission control for the daily briefing report. There were several teams on Earth, an army of specialists in the field of engineering, physics, geology, biochemistry, astronomy and linguistics, impatiently waiting, ready to decipher and evaluate the data provided by the Martian team. Of course, everything was handled with the highest level of classified information — top secret! The peoples of the world should be well prepared by their governments because careless revelation to the public may cause mayhem. The other way around, the astronauts relied on the breakdown of the analyzed data sent back from Earth. Based on that valuable information, interpretation and recommendation, the Martian team may make their best decision in upcoming situations on who, where, when, and what to do.

The Cosmic Library was more than just a repository of knowledge; it was a testament to the Martian civilization's incredible achievements and their unyielding desire to ensure their legacy lived on. As the team prepared to leave the chamber, they knew they had only scratched the surface of what this ancient civilization had to offer. The discoveries they made in the Cosmic Library would not only reshape humanity's understanding of Mars but also pave the way for future explorations and technological advancements.

With hearts and minds full of newfound knowledge, the astronauts set their sights on deciphering the secrets of the gateway, ready to unlock the next chapter in their extraordinary journey on Mars.

Chapter 10: Love and Rivalry

Clear-cut conditions or not?

The dim light of the pyramid chamber cast elongated shadows on the stone walls. Sophie stood near an alien stone face, its enigmatic eyes still haunting her thoughts. Ivan watched her from across the room. Their connection had deepened since their arrival on Mars — a shared secret that transcended the mission.

Sophie traced the carvings on the stone face, her fingers brushing over symbols that seemed to pulse with energy. Ivan approached, his footsteps silent on the dusty floor. "Sophie," he said softly, "we're part of something greater than ourselves."

She turned to him, her eyes searching his. "Ivan," she whispered, "what if love is forbidden? What if our feelings put everything in danger and we neglect our duties?"

He took her hand, the touch sending a jolt through both of them. "Forbidden love," he said, "is often the most powerful."

Wei harbored her own desires. Inspite of the previous disappointment after their romantic intermezzo on The Ares Horizon, Klaus had captured her heart. She watched Sophie and Ivan from a distance.

One evening, as the crew gathered around the holographic display, Wei challenged Emily. "Klaus," she said, her voice steady, "who will you choose?"

Klaus hesitated, torn between the two women. "Our mission," he said, "is to unlock the gateway. But our hearts…" He glanced at Sophie and Ivan. "Our hearts have other plans."

Sophie leaned against Ivan, their love a beacon in the darkness. "We'll find a way," she said. "To unlock the gateway and protect our fragile world."

But Wei's eyes held determination. "And if love is the key," she said, "then I won't give up without a fight."

As the pyramid whispered its secrets, the astronauts grappled with their desires, their destinies, and the cosmic forces that bound them together.

The atmosphere within the Martian pyramid grew increasingly charged, not just due to the mysteries they were unraveling but also because of the complex web of emotions among the crew members. The interactions between Wei, Emily and Klaus became a focal point of both camaraderie and tension.

From the beginning, it was clear that there was a unique connection between Wei and Klaus. Their mutual respect and shared scientific passions created a strong foundation for their relationship.

As an engineer and linguist, Wei's sharp intellect and enthusiasm for discovery were matched by Klaus's analytical mind and depth in biology and chemistry. They often spent long hours working together, their conversations seamlessly shifting from professional to personal.

Klaus admired Wei's dedication and ingenuity. Her ability to decipher the ancient Martian symbols and understand their technology impressed him deeply. Over time, he found himself drawn to her not just as a colleague but as a confidante and friend.

Emily initially kept to herself and concentrated on her work. However, as she witnessed the growing closeness between Wei and Klaus, she began to develop feelings for Klaus herself. Emily's fascination with Klaus' intellect and his methodical approach to her discoveries developed into a deeper emotional connection. Her quiet strength and independence were qualities that Klaus admired. However, he focused more on his professional relationship with Wei.

The first signs of rivalry appeared again, as Emily began to spend more time with Klaus. She often sought his opinion on geological findings, framing her questions in a way that highlighted her own insights. Klaus, appreciating her expertise, welcomed these discussions, unaware of the emotional undertones they carried.

Compared to Sophie's outspoken nature, Emily's British character was more reserved. She relied on her intellectual prowess to capture Klaus's attention. Her conversations with him were deeply engaging, often leaving Klaus contemplating their discussions long after they had ended.

Wei noticed Emily's increasing presence and felt a pang of insecurity. Her connection with Klaus was strong, but Emily's quiet persistence began to create doubts. Wei confided in Commander Harris, who had become a mentor and supportive figure for her.

Commander Harris said:"Wei, you and Klaus have a genuine bond. Don't let Emily's actions undermine your confidence. Speak to Klaus, be honest about your feelings."

One evening, after a particularly intense day of exploration, Wei decided to address the situation. She found Klaus in one of the chambers, examining a set of hieroglyphs.

Wei approached Klaus and asked him:"Klaus, can we talk?"

Klaus looked up, sensing the seriousness in her tone. "Of course, Wei. What's on your mind?"

Wei took a deep breath. "I've noticed Emily has been spending a lot of time with you. It's been bothering me because… well, because I care about you."

Klaus's eyes softened. "Wei I had no idea. I value our time together and what we've built. Emily is a colleague and a friend, but you… you mean more to me than that. Wei – weida!" Klaus made a punning in Chinese with Wei's first name, because 威 "Wei" means "prestige" and 伟大 "weida" means "great".

As fate would have it, Emily walked in on their conversation. She had come to discuss some recent geological findings with Klaus, but the sight of Wei and Klaus in such a heartfelt moment stopped her in her tracks.

Emily interrupted with her comment: "I'm sorry, I didn't mean to intrude."

Wei turned to Emily, her expression a mix of vulnerability and determination. "Emily, we need to talk. This situation… it's affecting all of us."

Emily nodded, understanding the gravity of the moment. "You're right. Let's talk."

The three of them sat down, the tension in the air palpable.

"Wei, Klaus… I need to be honest. I've developed feelings for Klaus. But I never intended to come between you two. My feelings grew out of admiration and respect, but I see now that I've crossed a line."

Klaus looked at both women, his voice steady. "We're a team, and our mission is too important to let personal feelings create divisions. Emily, I respect you and value your contributions, but my heart lies with Wei."

The conversation, though difficult, brought a sense of clarity and mutual respect. Emily, recognizing the strength of Wei and Klaus's bond, decided to step back and refocus her energy on the mission. She and Wei reached an understanding, agreeing to support each other as colleagues and friends.

Wei said to Emily:"Emily, thank you for being honest. I respect you too, and I hope we can move forward without tension."

Emily answered:"Absolutely, Wei. Let's focus on what brought us here. The Martian secrets are far more important than our personal feelings." That's what she said, but she secretly disagreed and didn't want to give up so quickly. Behind her reserved British manner, which enveloped her like a protective shell, she revealed herself to be a combative girl who was ready to vie with Wei for Klaus. All she needed was patience and the right moment to attack with her love arrows.

Klaus, presently relieved by the resolution, felt a renewed sense of unity among the team. He was grateful for the honesty and maturity with which both women handled the situation.

Rekindled Hearts

The Martian pyramid held many secrets, but none as intricate and personal as the emotions among its explorers. The resolution between Wei, Emily and Klaus had brought a temporary peace, but the undercurrents of attraction and unspoken feelings lingered. As the team delved deeper into the mysteries of the ancient Martian civilization, the evolving relationships among them took an unexpected turn.

Despite stepping back, Emily's feelings for Klaus didn't simply vanish. She respected the bond between Klaus and Wei but couldn't ignore the connection she felt. Emily channeled her emotions into her work, hoping to prove herself not just as a capable scientist but as someone worthy of Klaus's admiration.

Emily immersed herself in her geological research, uncovering significant insights about the Martian landscape and its history. Her dedication and breakthroughs garnered respect from the entire team, including Klaus.

One sol, while exploring a newly revealed chamber, Emily stumbled upon a series of carvings that seemed to depict the Martian understanding of planetary geology and resource management. Realizing the importance of her find, she immediately sought out Klaus.

Emily involved him as followed:"Klaus, you need to see this. These carvings — they illustrate the Martians' methods for harnessing planetary resources. It's like nothing we've ever seen."

Klaus, intrigued by Emily's excitement, followed her to the chamber. As they examined the carvings together, their shared passion for discovery reignited the connection between them.

Klaus enthusiastically answered:"This is incredible, Emily. Your insights could revolutionize our understanding of Martian geology and resource utilization."

Their collaboration on this project brought them closer, reminding Klaus of the intellectual synergy and chemistry he shared with Emily. The more time they spent together, the more Klaus found himself drawn to her resilience and brilliance.

Meanwhile, Wei's responsibilities continued to grow. Her expertise in engineering and linguistics was crucial for deciphering the Martian technology and symbols. As she became more engrossed in her work, the time she spent with Klaus began to diminish.

Wei remained committed to their mission but couldn't help noticing the renewed closeness between Klaus and Emily. Though she trusted Klaus, she felt a pang of insecurity, worried that her relationship with him was becoming secondary to their scientific endeavors.

One evening, as the team gathered to discuss their findings, Emily presented her latest research on the geological carvings. Her eloquence and depth of knowledge impressed everyone, but it was Klaus who looked at her with newfound admiration.

Klaus addressed words of praise to Emily:"Emily, your work is groundbreaking. The clarity and detail you've provided offer new perspectives on the capabilities of the Martians. I'm genuinely amazed."

Wei, observing the interaction, felt a mix of pride and apprehension. After the meeting, she approached Klaus, wanting to address her concerns.

Wei dared to say the following words to Klaus without fear of losing face:"Klaus, I've noticed you and Emily have been working closely together. I understand the importance of collaboration, but I can't help feeling we're drifting apart."

Klaus, taken aback by Wei's honesty, took her hand. "Wei, your work is indispensable, and I respect you deeply. But I've realized that my connection with Emily is also strong. I need to be honest about my feelings."

Emily's Patience Rewarded

Klaus's words echoed in Wei's mind as she processed the reality of their situation. Understanding the depth of Klaus's feelings for Emily, she decided to step back, respecting his honesty and their mutual desire to prioritize their mission.

With Wei's acceptance, Klaus felt free to explore his relationship with Emily without guilt. He sought her out later that evening, eager to express his true feelings.

Klaus clarified:"Emily, I've come to realize that my admiration for you goes beyond professional respect. You inspire me in ways I hadn't fully acknowledged before."

Emily's eyes widened, hope and joy mingling in her expression. "Klaus, I've felt the same way. I've tried to respect your relationship with Wei, but my feelings for you have only grown stronger."

Their conversation marked the beginning of a new chapter in their relationship. Klaus and Emily spent more time together, their bond deepening with each shared discovery and heartfelt conversation. They supported each other's work, combining their strengths to unravel the pyramid's secrets.

Klaus and Emily's relationship blossomed in the Martian landscape. They shared quiet moments under the dome of the pyramid, discussing their dreams and aspirations. Their connection, forged in the crucible of exploration and intellectual partnership, became a source of strength for both.

Wei, though initially heartbroken, found solace in her work and the supportive presence of her other teammates. She admired Emily and Klaus's relationship, recognizing the genuine connection they shared. Wei channeled her energy into uncovering more about the Martian civilization, finding fulfillment in the mission that had brought them all together.

The love and rivalry among the astronauts had tested their resolve and commitment to each other. Through honesty, respect, and understanding, they navigated their personal challenges, emerging stronger as individuals and as a team.

Emily's persistence and intellectual passion ultimately won Klaus's heart, creating a partnership that was both romantic and professional. Their bond, alongside the camaraderie of their fellow explorers, fortified their mission, preparing them for the monumental discoveries yet to come.

Chapter 11: "MacGyverisms"

First Challenge: The Holographic Guardian

An astronaut has to combine many qualities in one person. He or she should be a bit of everything: medical doctor, pilot, engineer, scientist, foreign language speaker, endurance athlete.

The motivation to become an astronaut for some people may have begun with the identification of the fictional film character "MacGyver"® from the 1980s. This guy would manage to keep a cool head in sheer hopeless situations and to improvise, i.e. to find creative solutions and use objects in unconventional ways to solve problems.

Thus, the six astronauts stood at the entrance of a newly discovered chamber deep within the Martian pyramid. The dim light from their headlamps flickered across the ancient walls, revealing intricate carvings and alien hieroglyphs. The air was thick with anticipation and the faint smell of dust and metal.

"Careful, everyone," Commander Harris warned. "We don't know what we're dealing with here."

As they stepped into the chamber, the ground beneath them shifted. The heavy stone door slammed shut behind them, trapping them inside. The walls began to tremble, and a low humming noise filled the room. Suddenly, a holographic projection of an alien guardian materialized in the center of the chamber, blocking their path to a mysterious pedestal at the far end.

"We need to find a way to deactivate that guardian," Emily said, scanning the room for clues.

The chamber's tremors intensified, and small pieces of debris began to fall from the ceiling. The hum of the holographic guardian grew louder, a warning of its impending attack?

Emily, eyes wide with determination, shouted over the noise, "We need to work fast. Klaus, find anything that looks like it could be a control panel. Ivan, see if you can figure out how this guardian is powered."

Klaus examined the hologram. "It's likely controlled by some kind of ancient mechanism. We just need to figure out how to access it."

Sophie, sweating from the mounting tension, ran her fingers along the walls, searching for hidden mechanisms. "There must be something we're missing," she muttered to herself.

"Over here!" Sophie's voice cut through the chaos, drawing the team's attention to the concealed panel she had discovered. The alien symbols glowed faintly, promising a solution if they could just unlock its secrets. "There are some alien symbols and what looks like a keypad."

Commander Harris and Wei hurried to her side. "Let's see if we can make sense of this," Commander Harris said, wiping dust from his helmet's visor.

Wei, who had studied ancient languages and symbology, quickly got to work. "These symbols... they're not just numbers. They seem to represent a sequence of actions or commands. It's a code."

Ivan, meanwhile, knelt beside the holographic guardian, studying its projection. "I think it's linked to the pedestal," he theorized. "If we can disable the control mechanism, the guardian should deactivate. But we don't have the right tools to hack it."

Inguinity and Improvisation Required

Emily crouched near the alien control panel. She rummaged through their supplies. Her gloved hands worked swiftly, pulling out wires, batteries, and a small handheld scanner from their equipment cache. The Martian dust clung to her suit as he muttered to herself. Emily began to dismantle the small handheld scanner. "If we can interface this scanner with the keypad, we might be able to decode and input the right sequence."

Sophie nodded, quickly understanding the plan. "We'll need to strip some wires and reroute the power. Ivan, can you help with that?" Sophie, ever resourceful, pulled out a small multi-tool from her belt. "We might not have the proper tools, but we can improvise. Let's see what we can come up with."

Ivan nodded, his engineering background kicking in. "On it."

Using the multi-tool, Sophie carefully removed the scanner's casing, exposing its delicate components. Ivan stripped wires from their communication devices, connecting the scanner's circuitry to the keypad. The group worked in tense silence, their movements precise and coordinated.

Commander Harris and Wei gathered around the panel, using their knowledge of ancient languages and alien technology to decipher the symbols. Meanwhile, Sophie and Ivan began dismantling their equipment, searching for anything that could be repurposed.

Klaus kept a lookout, his eyes scanning the chamber for any signs of further instability. "Hurry," he urged. "The guardian's hum is getting louder."

Wei and Commander Harris worked together, deciphering the alien symbols. "It's a sequence of prime numbers," Wei realized. "If we input them in the right order, it should deactivate the guardian."

With the device assembled and the code deciphered, Commander Harris stepped forward. "All right, moment of truth. Let's hope this works."

Commander Harris nodded. "Let's do this."

Sophie connected the makeshift decoder to the keypad, her hands steady despite the high stakes. She entered the prime number sequence, each symbol lighting up in turn.

The device hummed to life, and the symbols on the keypad lit up in sequence. For a moment, the room was filled with tense silence. Then, the holographic guardian flickered and disappeared. The ground stopped shaking, and the walls ceased their tremors. The chamber fell silent once more, leaving the team standing in awe of their accomplishment.

With the guardian deactivated, the team approached the pedestal. On it lay a small, intricately carved box. Ivan carefully opened it, revealing a collection of data crystal containing valuable information about the pyramid's builders.

"We did it," Sophie said, a smile of relief spreading across her face. "We improvised and overcame the challenge."

Commander Harris placed a hand on her shoulder. "That's what being an astronaut is all about — thinking on your feet and working together. Great job, everyone. I love it when a plan comes together!"

As they left the chamber, the team felt a renewed sense of camaraderie and confidence. They had faced the unknown and emerged victorious, proving that with ingenuity and teamwork, they could overcome any obstacle the Martian pyramid threw their way.

And so, they pressed on — their improvised creation bridging worlds, unlocking secrets. A "MacGyver" would have been proud.

Second Challenge: The Resonant Trap

Based on the data crystal, which was found by Ivan, they held a kind of blueprint of the pyramid in their hands. Therefore, they ventured into a new section of the pyramid, where an elaborate network of bridges connected multiple chambers suspended high above the ground.

The team was in high spirits, with Sophie and Ivan leading the way. Their excitement was palpable, and in an effort to lift everyone's spirits further, they began singing an old Earth song. The melody echoed through the vast, cavernous space of the pyramid, creating an otherworldly symphony.

As the team crossed one of the longer, more delicate bridges, Sophie and Ivan's synchronized steps inadvertently created a lockstep. The rhythm of their footsteps, combined with their singing, set up a resonant frequency that matched the natural frequency of the bridge. The structure began to vibrate alarmingly, causing the team to halt in their tracks.

Commander Harris, sensing danger, shouted for everyone to stop. But it was too late. The bridge's support mechanisms started to fail, and the vibrations triggered an ancient Martian security system. The bridge retracted rapidly, and the team found themselves trapped in a small, enclosed chamber at the far end of the bridge.

The walls of the chamber began to close. A hidden mechanism had been activated and had trapped them. The team had to act quickly to avoid being crushed.

Improvisation Takes Shape

Commander Harris assessed the situation quickly. "We need to disable the mechanism that's closing these walls. Emily, see if you can find any control panels or access points."

Emily nodded and, along with Wei, began to examine the walls and floor for any signs of a control system. Meanwhile, Klaus analyzed the structural integrity of the chamber, looking for weak points that could be exploited.

Sophie and Ivan, feeling guilty for their earlier mistake, were determined to make amends. Ivan, an expert in electrical systems, suggested a plan. "We can use the metal components from our equipment and suits to create a mechanical solution."

Working together, the team quickly gathered materials. They dismantled some non-essential parts of their suits, such as belt buckles and metal fasteners. Ivan used his multitool to shape and modify the metal pieces into makeshift wedges and levers. Klaus, with his background in structural engineering, guided the assembly of these components into a jamming device.

Time was running out as the walls continued to close in. Sophie, with her steady hands, positioned the wedges and levers at critical points where the walls met. Emily found a narrow gap that seemed to house part of the closing mechanism.

"We need to manually stop this mechanism," Emily said, her voice urgent. "If we can jam it, we can buy ourselves some time."

Klaus and Ivan worked together to insert the wedges into the gap Emily had found. Using their combined strength, they levered the metal pieces into place, creating a physical block that halted the movement of the walls. The grinding noise of the mechanism trying to close the walls grew louder, but the makeshift jamming device held firm.

The walls stopped closing, and the pressure in the chamber stabilized. The team quickly assessed their surroundings, searching for an exit. Wei spotted a small panel that seemed to control the door mechanism.

"Here! Help me open this," she called out. Commander Harris and Sophie rushed over, using their tools to pry open the panel. Inside, they found a series of gears and levers.

"We need to manually operate this to open the door," Commander Harris said. "Emily, can you figure out the sequence?"

Emily nodded, her mind racing. "Give me a moment." She carefully studied the gears, aligning them in a specific order. With a final push, the door mechanism clicked, and the hidden door slid open, revealing a passage to safety.

As they regrouped outside the chamber, breathing sighs of relief, Commander Harris commended the team for their quick thinking and resourcefulness. "We made it out because we worked together and used our skills creatively. That's true "MacGyverism"."

Sophie and Ivan exchanged grateful glances. "We'll be more careful next time," Sophie said, smiling despite the tension.

Wei added, "This experience just proves how much we rely on each other. We'll face whatever comes next together."

The team continued their exploration of the Martian pyramid, their bond stronger than ever, ready to tackle whatever challenges lay ahead.

Third Challenge: The Shifting Floor

The team continued their exploration of the Martian pyramid, unaware that another test of their ingenuity lay just ahead. They entered a vast, dimly lit chamber filled with intricate machinery and alien hieroglyphs. The room was silent except for the occasional hum of technology.

As they moved deeper into the chamber, a loud click echoed through the room. Suddenly, the floor began to shift beneath their feet, splitting into sections that started to rise and fall, creating an uneven, shifting landscape. It was a trap designed to disorient and separate them.

Separated by the moving floor, the team struggled to stay together. Commander Harris, Emily, and Klaus ended up on one side of the chamber, while Wei, Sophie, and Ivan were on the other. The shifting floor made it impossible to cross back.

To make matters worse, the ceiling began to descend slowly, threatening to crush them if they didn't find a way out quickly. The team needed to deactivate the trap and reunite before it was too late.

The Makeshift Solution

Commander Harris shouted instructions over the noise of the shifting floor. "Emily, Klaus, look for any control panels or switches! Wei, Sophie, Ivan, see if you can find anything on your side!"

Emily and Klaus began to search the walls for any signs of a control mechanism. Meanwhile, Wei noticed a series of glowing symbols on the floor near her. "I think these symbols might be a clue!" she called out.

Sophie examined the symbols closely. "They look like some kind of puzzle. If we can match them correctly, it might deactivate the trap."

Ivan, ever resourceful, suggested a plan. "We need to communicate the symbols we see to each other and figure out the correct sequence. Use the reflective surfaces on our equipment to signal each other."

Using pieces of their suits and tools, the team created makeshift mirrors and reflective surfaces. They began signaling each other across the room, sharing the symbols they saw.

Emily and Klaus found a series of corresponding symbols on their side. "We need to match these symbols in the right order," Emily deduced. "It's like a combination lock."

As the ceiling continued to descend, the team worked quickly, signaling back and forth to align the symbols correctly. Sophie and Ivan carefully pressed the symbols on their side, while Emily and Klaus did the same.

The floor continued to shift, making it difficult to maintain their balance. Commander Harris kept everyone focused. "Stay calm and steady. We've got this."

With the symbols correctly aligned, a loud click echoed through the chamber. The shifting floor suddenly stopped, and the descending ceiling began to retract. The trap had been deactivated.

Relieved, the team regrouped in the center of the chamber. "Great work, everyone," Commander Harris praised. "Our quick thinking and teamwork saved us again."

Sophie and Ivan exchanged a high-five. "That was close, but we did it," Sophie said, grinning.

Wei added, "We make a pretty good team. Let's hope we don't have to solve too many more puzzles like that."

The team continued their exploration, more confident in their ability to overcome the challenges the Martian pyramid had in store for them. They knew that as long as they worked together and used their ingenuity, they could face any obstacle that came their way.

Chapter 12: The Mysteries of Laniakea

The Discovery

The next Martian pyramid's chamber was bathed in an otherworldly light, casting intricate shadows that seemed to dance and shift as the astronauts delved deeper into its mysteries. However, Commander Harris did not take part in the discovery tour today, as he suffered from space sickness or space adaptation syndrome (SAS), which is similar to motion sickness and can be triggered by the effects of microgravity or changes in gravity. Although Mars has about 38% of Earth's gravity, the transition to this different gravitational environment after being in microgravity (as in a spacecraft) or Earth's gravity can cause a range of symptoms such as nausea and vomiting, disorientation, headcahces, loss of appetite, and fatigue. Therefore, he tried to recover by remaining at the habitat today and left the exploration to his team members, which were eager to do their job.

The Cosmic Library had revealed many secrets, but none more intriguing than the map of Laniakea — the vast galactic supercluster that included the Milky Way.

Klaus studied the holographic display, his eyes wide with wonder. "Laniakea," he murmured. "It means "immeasurable heaven" in Hawaiian. This... this is a map of our entire cosmic neighborhood."

Emily peered at the intricate web of galaxies. "It's breathtaking," she said softly. "A vast network of stars and planets, all interconnected. What could the Martians have been doing with this?"

As they continued to study the map, the pyramid seemed to respond to their curiosity. Symbols and glyphs illuminated, revealing more about the Martian civilization's purpose. Sophie traced her fingers over the glowing inscriptions, her mind racing to translate the ancient language.

"The Martians were not just explorers," she said, her voice filled with awe. "They were guardians of knowledge, curators of the universe's secrets."

Ivan, standing beside her, nodded. "They saw themselves as stewards of the cosmos, preserving and protecting the balance of life and energy across galaxies."

The map of Laniakea wasn't just a static display — it was a dynamic, living network. Lines of light pulsed and shifted, showing the flow of energy and information between galaxies. Wei, her eyes bright with fascination, pointed to a particularly vibrant node.

"This," she said, "this is the heart of Laniakea. It's where the energy converges, a nexus of power and knowledge. The Martians must have used this to monitor and maintain the stability of the supercluster."

The Hub of Harmony

The team focused on the central hub of Laniakea, where the energy flows converged. The pyramid revealed more details, showing structures and machinery far beyond anything they had imagined. Klaus, his scientific curiosity piqued, leaned in closer.

"These are advanced beyond our wildest dreams," he said. "Energy management systems, data repositories, communication networks — it's like the central nervous system of the supercluster."

Emily's eyes widened as she realized the implications. "They weren't just monitoring the galaxies," she said. "They were actively managing them, ensuring harmony and balance."

The pyramid's light intensified, drawing their attention to a specific point on the map — a distant galaxy on the fringes of Laniakea. Sophie squinted at the glowing symbols, deciphering their meaning.

"This appears to be a distress signal," she said in an urgent voice. "A galaxy is in trouble, its energy flows have been disrupted."

Ivan's face hardened with determination. "We need to investigate," he said. "The Martians entrusted us with their knowledge. It's our duty to continue their work."

The team gathered their equipment, preparing to explore this new frontier. The pyramid's energy pulsed around them, guiding and supporting their efforts. As they reviewed their plans, they felt a profound sense of responsibility and purpose.

"We're not just explorers anymore," Klaus said, his voice firm. "We're guardians, following in the footsteps of the Martians."

As they studied the holographic map, they noticed that the heart of Laniakea was a vast, luminous chamber filled with holographic displays and advanced machinery. The air thrummed with energy, and the walls pulsed with a soft, rhythmic light.

"This is it," Wei said, her voice filled with awe. "The heart of Laniakea. The Nexus, the connecting point of an immeasurable number of galaxies."

Emily tapped her chin thoughtfully. "We need to understand the nature of the disruption," she said. "Is it natural or artificial? And what's causing it?"

Klaus nodded in agreement. "Let's start by isolating the source of the disturbance. We can use the pyramid's analytical tools to get a clearer picture."

Using the pyramid's advanced technology, the astronauts began to dissect the data. Emily and Klaus worked on isolating the specific wavelengths and energy signatures, while Sophie and Wei translated the accompanying glyphs for any historical context.

"It's an artificial interference," Emily said after a while. "Someone or something is causing this disruption."

Sophie, decoding more glyphs, added, "It seems to be linked to an ancient Martian outpost. They left behind machines to manage the energy flows, but something has gone wrong."

With the nature of the disruption identified, the team began to devise a plan. Ivan, ever the strategist, outlined their approach.

"We need to restore the balance," he said. "We'll start by pinpointing the exact location of the outpost and assessing the damage."

Wei agreed. "We should also prepare for any potential challenges. If this is a Martian installation, we might face security measures or malfunctions."

The pyramid's technology allowed for remote interfacing with the distant outpost. Emily and Klaus set up a secure link, while Sophie and Wei monitored the data streams.

"We're in," Klaus said, his fingers flying over the controls. "The systems are still operational, but there's significant damage to the energy regulators."

Emily frowned. "Can we fix it remotely?"

The initial scans revealed that many of the issues could be resolved remotely. The team began to reroute energy flows and repair damaged circuits using the pyramid's advanced interface.

"It's like performing surgery from millions of light-years away," Ivan remarked, his eyes glued to the holographic display.

Wei added, "We need to be precise. One wrong move, and we could cause more harm than good."

Overcoming Obstacles

As they worked, unexpected challenges arose. Automated defenses activated, mistaking their interference for an attack. The team had to carefully navigate these systems, using the pyramid's knowledge to deactivate them without causing further damage.

Sophie, her fingers deftly manipulating the controls, said, "These defenses are advanced, but we have the Martian knowledge on our side. We can do this."

After hours of intense work, the energy flows began to stabilize. The distress signal faded, replaced by a steady, harmonious pulse.

"It's a delicate balance," Klaus said. "We need to align the energy streams perfectly, or we risk causing even more disruption."

As they worked, the situation grew more urgent. The energy flows were becoming increasingly unstable, threatening to cascade into a catastrophic collapse. Ivan and Wei moved with precision, adjusting the machinery and fine-tuning the energy outputs.

"We're close," Wei said, her voice tense. "Just a little more."

With a final adjustment, the energy flows stabilized, and the distress signal ceased. The team let out a collective sigh of relief, their hearts pounding with adrenaline.

"We did it," Sophie said, a triumphant smile spreading across her face. "We saved the galaxy."

"Yes, indeed. We did it," Klaus said, a triumphant smile spreading across his face. "The outpost is back online, and the energy flows are stable."

Emily let out a sigh of relief. "The galaxy is safe, for now. We've honored the Martian legacy."

As they stood in the heart of the pyramid, the light around them pulsed in a rhythm that felt almost like a heartbeat — a silent acknowledgment of their achievement. They had proven themselves worthy of the Martian trust, becoming true guardians of the cosmos.

"We have a responsibility," Ivan said, his voice filled with resolve. "To protect and preserve the balance of the universe."

"And to continue learning," Emily added, her eyes shining with determination. "To explore and understand the mysteries of Laniakea and beyond."

With their mission in Laniakea complete for now, the team prepared to return to their habitat, their hearts filled with a new sense of purpose. The journey ahead was uncertain, but they knew they were ready for whatever challenges lay in store.

As they stepped back from the holographic display, the pyramid whispered its final words of wisdom: "Knowledge is the light that guides us through the darkness. Be the guardians of the universe, and let your light shine brightly."

And so, the astronauts returned to their base, ready to face the future with courage and determination, their bond stronger than ever as they embarked on their next great adventure. Commander Harris's health condidition had improved significantly in the meantime.

Chapter 13: Cracking the Code

The Gateway Mechanism

On next sol, on one of the plinths, Commander Harris found a detailed schematic of the pyramid itself. At its center was a depiction of the large circular gateway they had seen in the carvings outside.

"Look at this," Commander Harris called out. "This seems to be a blueprint for the gateway. If we can decipher this, we might be able to understand how to activate it."

Klaus joined him. "And if we can activate the gateway, it could lead us to other locations — or even other worlds."

As they explored further, they found another section of the chamber dedicated to the guardian figures. Holographic projections showed the guardians in action, defending key sites from threats. These guardians were not just symbolic; they were advanced constructs, possibly robotic or bio-mechanical, designed to protect the Martian civilization's most valuable assets.

Emily, studying the projections, remarked:"These guardians were sophisticated security systems. They could be the reason why this pyramid and its knowledge have remained intact for so long."

Near the end of the chamber, they found a large, ornate door covered in hieroglyphs and carvings. The door seemed to pulsate with a faint, rhythmic light, as if it were alive.

"This must lead to something even more significant," Commander Harris said, placing his hand on the door. "We need to figure out how to open it."

Wei, examining the hieroglyphs, noticed a pattern. "I think it's another sequence, like the one we used to activate the plinths. Let's try to decipher it."

Working together, the team carefully pressed the hieroglyphs in the correct order. The door responded with a deep, resonant chime and slowly began to open, revealing a glowing chamber beyond.

As they stepped into the new chamber, their headlamps illuminated a sight that took their breath away: a massive, intricately carved structure that seemed to pulse with energy. In the center of the room was the gateway, a large, circular portal that shimmered with an otherworldly light.

Commander Harris turned to his team, his voice filled with awe. "We've just scratched the surface. This gateway could be the key to unlocking the mysteries of the Martian civilization and perhaps even the secrets of the universe itself."

With a mixture of excitement and reverence, the team prepared to delve deeper into the heart of the pyramid, ready to uncover the ultimate secrets of the ancient Martians.

Holographic displays flickered to life — images of Martian cities, starships, and beings of light. The hieroglyphs pulsed, revealing equations that defied earthly physics.

Sophie touched a stone face. "What do you want from us?" she asked silently.

And the stone face answered — in their minds, in their souls. It spoke of cosmic cycles, of ascension, and of a choice. The pyramid was a gateway not only to Mars but to the stars themselves.

As they explored further, they found smaller chambers branching off from the main hall. Each room held artifacts, from tools and weapons to what appeared to be scrolls made of a metallic substance.

Sophie, examining one of the scrolls, called out, "These might contain their records. We need to take them back to the base for analysis."

Ivan agreed, carefully packing the scrolls. "We'll need to handle them with care. They could be fragile after all this time."

In one of the deeper chambers, they discovered what appeared to be a throne room. A large, ornate chair stood at the center, facing a massive wall carved with a detailed map of the stars.

Emily, captivated by the map, traced the constellations with her fingers. "This could be their navigation system, their guide to using the gateway."

Wei nodded, her eyes reflecting the glow of the carvings. "We need to recreate this. It might show us how to activate the machine."

Klaus, standing by the throne, found a series of buttons and levers embedded in the armrests. "This throne might be the control center. If we can understand how it works, we might be able to operate the gateway."

Commander Harris, feeling a sense of urgency, addressed the team. "Let's document everything here and start working on decoding the controls. We're on the verge of something monumental."

Hours turned into days (or better: sols) as the team worked tirelessly, their initial awe giving way to a focused determination. Emily and Wei, now working seamlessly together, decoded the hieroglyphs while Klaus analyzed the chemical composition of the materials used.

Ivan and Sophie, their bond strengthening with each passing day, handled the physical aspects of the exploration, ensuring that every artifact was carefully preserved.

One evening, as the team gathered for a rare moment of rest, Commander Harris addressed them. "We've made incredible progress, but there's still much to uncover. Our mission is evolving. We're not just explorers; we're historians, scientists, and diplomats to another world."

The team nodded, a sense of unity and purpose filling the room. They were not just uncovering the past; they were bridging the gap between two worlds, two civilizations.

Their mission had evolved from exploration to a quest for knowledge, a journey that would take them beyond the confines of Mars and into the vast unknown. Together, they would continue to push the boundaries of human achievement, inspired by the legacy of the ancient Martian civilization.

The Celestial Codex

The chamber hummed with energy as the crew gathered around Astraeus — the stone face that had become both their guide and their confidant. Sophie traced the intricate carvings, her fingers brushing over symbols that seemed to pulse with life. Ivan stood beside her, their love a silent promise in the face of cosmic revelation.

"Astraeus," Sophie whispered, "what lies within the Celestial Codex?"

Sophie deliberately referred to Greek mythology. Astraeus is a Titan god associated with the dusk and the stars. He is the son of Crius and Eurybia, and he is often linked with the evening and the winds. Astraeus is also the father of the Anemoi (the wind gods) and the stars, through his union with Eos, the goddess of the dawn.

Therefore, "Astraeus" literally means "starry" or "of the stars", highlighting his connection to celestial bodies and phenomena.

The stone face responded, not with words, but with images and symbols: Martian cities bathed in starlight, beings of pure energy dancing among the constellations — the civilization that had once thrived on this desolate planet. They had transcended physical form, their consciousness merging with the very fabric of the cosmos.

"The Codex," Astraeus conveyed, "holds the culmination of their wisdom — their legacy."

Emily stepped forward. "Faster-than-light travel," she said. "The key to unlocking the stars. Imagine what humanity could achieve — a leap beyond our solar system."

Klaus nodded. "But the Codex demands sacrifice," he said. "What price are we prepared to pay for such knowledge?"

Sophie looked at Ivan. "Our love," she said, "is a force that transcends cosmic boundaries. But what if it's not enough?"

They discovered a crystalline structure - the Celestial Codex itself. Its facets refracted the light, casting rainbows into the chamber. Emily's fingers hovered over the surface, hesitant yet eager. The crystal's facets were not merely decorative, but part of a complex, multidimensional puzzle.

"What do you make of this?" asked Commander Harris.

Emily's eyes scanned the grid. "These numbers... they're not random. There's a pattern here."

Klaus, as a biochemist with a knack for mathematics, nodded. "You're right, Emily. This reminds me of something familiar."

Sophie pointed out several sequences. "Look at these: 1, 1, 2, 3, 5, 8, 13... It's a Fibonacci sequence."

"A Fibonacci sequence?" Wei inquired.

"It's a series where each number is the sum of the two preceding ones," Klaus explained. "It's found in nature, in the arrangement of leaves, the pattern of flowers, even the spirals of galaxies."

Ivan studied the panel more closely. "If this is a Fibonacci sequence, then maybe the key lies in completing or identifying these sequences."

Emily, always quick to pick up on mathematical clues, suggested, "Let's test that theory. We need to identify if any of the numbers in the grid are missing or out of place. If we can correct or complete the sequence, it might trigger a mechanism."

They all gathered around the panel, examining the numbers. It became clear that some numbers were missing from the expected sequence. They started to fill in the blanks, each astronaut contributing their knowledge and expertise.

Commander Harris called out the numbers as they filled them in: "1, 1, 2, 3, 8, 13, 34, 55..."

Sophie, writing down the numbers as Commander Harris called them out, noticed something. "Wait, there's a missing number here. Between 8 and 13, we need 5."

"Exactly," said Klaus. "And here, between 13 and 34, we need 21."

Wei tapped her chin thoughtfully. "So, we need to input these missing numbers into the grid."

Ivan began to press the corresponding symbols on the panel. They all held their breath as the final number was pressed.

In that moment, the crystal seemed to respond, the light within it shifting to reveal a hidden compartment. Inside, they found an ancient scroll, its surface covered with the same intricate patterns as the crystal.

"Looks like we did it," Ivan said, a smile spreading across his face.

Wei carefully unrolled the scroll, her eyes scanning the text.

"What secrets does the codex hold?" Emily murmured, her eyes reflecting the kaleidoscopic light.

"It says here," Wei said:"The gateway, the alignment of worlds. The cosmic union - everything leads to a decision."

Klaus looked at Wei:"Perhaps the codex will not only reveal knowledge, but also our destiny?" he asked.

Emily traced the complex patterns of the codex. "It's not just about knowledge," she said. "It's a cosmic equation - a delicate balance."

Klaus nodded. "To unleash its power," he explained, "we must sacrifice something precious - a life force."

Sophie looked at Ivan, her love a silent promise. "But whose life?" she whispered.

Chapter 14: The Betrayal

The atmosphere inside the Martian pyramid grew tense as the astronauts deciphered more about the enigmatic gateway. The realization dawned on them that activating the gateway might require a significant sacrifice, potentially putting someone's life at risk. The weight of this revelation hung heavy over the team, causing unease and sparking underlying tensions.

Uncovering the Gateway's Secret

After days of intensive study, Wei and Emily managed to decode the final instructions for activating the gateway. The glyphs revealed that the gateway demanded a "life energy" transfer to function — essentially, a living being would have to step into the gateway to power it, possibly never returning.

Commander Harris gathered the team. "We have a tough decision to make. This gateway could be the key to unimaginable knowledge, but the cost is high. Someone has to enter it, and we don't know what will happen once they do."

Ivan stepped forward with resolute determination. "I'll do it. This is a once-in-a-lifetime opportunity, and if it means securing our future, then it's a risk worth taking."

Sophie's face paled at Ivan's declaration. They had grown close over the course of their mission, their bond deepening into a quiet, mutual affection. The thought of losing Ivan was unbearable to her.

The Night Before

That night, Sophie wrestled with her emotions. She couldn't stand the idea of Ivan sacrificing himself. Desperation gnawed at her, and she knew she had to act.

She sought out Wei, who was still working late into the night, meticulously organizing the data they had collected. Sophie's eyes narrowed as she observed the diminutive engineer, a plan forming in her mind.

The Act of Betrayal

The following day, as the team gathered in front of the gateway, tensions were high. Ivan stood ready, his expression a mixture of fear and determination.

Sophie, her mind racing, approached him. "Ivan, wait. We need to double-check the system. Let me just make sure everything is set."

Ivan nodded, trusting her implicitly. As Sophie moved to the control panel, she glanced at Wei, who was engrossed in calibrating some equipment. Sophie took a deep breath, her heart pounding, and made her move.

With a swift, practiced motion, she pushed Wei towards the gateway. The petite engineer stumbled, her eyes wide with shock and confusion.

"Sophie, what are you —" Wei's protest was cut short as she was propelled forward by the force of Sophie's push.

Wei's last words could hardly be heard. The others made out something like:"For humanity."

Ivan, realizing what was happening, lunged to stop her, but it was too late. The gateway's sensors activated, locking onto Wei. The ancient machine hummed to life, its power building as it drew energy from its captive.

The Aftermath

The room filled with a brilliant, otherworldly light as the gateway activated, its mechanisms whirring and glowing. The team watched in stunned silence as Wei was enveloped by the light, her form fading into the radiance.

"Sophie, what have you done?" Emily shouted, rushing to the control panel, desperately trying to reverse the process, but it was futile. The gateway had initiated, and Wei was gone.

Commander Harris grabbed Sophie, pulling her away from the controls. "Why, Sophie? Why did you do that?"

Sophie's eyes were wild with a mixture of fear and defiance. "I couldn't let Ivan go. I couldn't lose him. I... I just reacted."

Ivan, his face pale with shock and rage, stepped back from Sophie, unable to look at her. "You've condemned her, Sophie. We don't know what's on the other side. You acted out of selfishness and fear."

Emily, her voice trembling with anger, added, "You betrayed us all. We were a team, Sophie. You've broken that trust." Secretly, she was grateful to Sophie, as her rival for love to Klaus was gone now. She could not officially admit this, of course.

The rest of the team was left in disarray. The gateway remained active, its mysteries now overshadowed by the cost of its activation. They had gained access to untold knowledge, but at the price of their cohesion and the life of a trusted colleague.

Commander Harris, trying to regain some control over the situation, said, "We need to document everything that happened here. We need to understand the consequences of what we've done. But most importantly, we need to honor Wei by ensuring her sacrifice wasn't in vain."

Ivan turned to face the gateway, his expression resolute. "I won't let her sacrifice be for nothing. We need to find out what lies on the other side, and why the Martians built this gateway. We owe it to her — and to ourselves."

As the pyramid trembled, Sophie clung to Ivan. "We were meant to unlock the stars," she said. "But at what cost?"

Klaus's gaze met Sophie's. "Betrayal," he said, "is a wound that echoes through eternity."

The pyramid trembled as the gateway machine turned off.

Klaus stood before it, his heart heavy with remorse. Wei's sacrifice haunted him — the memory of her half-formed existence, suspended in cosmic limbo. Klaus stepped onto a stone platform. He sought redemption — for Wei, for Sophie, for all of humanity. His mind echoed with her last words: "For humanity." But what did it truly mean? Was sacrifice the only path to enlightenment?

Emily followed, her eyes alight with ambition. She had always hungered for knowledge — the kind that transcended textbooks and equations. The Codex had whispered secrets to her, promising answers to questions unasked. Leaving our world forever didn't daunt her; it thrilled her.

Sophie hesitated. Her love for Ivan warred with guilt — the guilt of betraying and of sacrificing Wei. She watched Wei vanish into the cosmic currents. But what lay beyond? Redemption? Answers? Or more heartache?

And so, within the heart of Mars, love and sacrifice collided — a cosmic dance that threatened to tear them apart.

Chapter 15: Wei's Journey

As the gateway's light enveloped Wei, she felt an intense sensation of being pulled in multiple directions simultaneously. The sensation was disorienting, as if her very essence was being stretched across the fabric of space-time. She could hear faint echoes of the Martian technology humming, harmonizing with an energy source far more ancient and powerful than anything she had ever encountered.

The Transition

Wei's vision blurred, then shifted to a kaleidoscope of colors, fractals spiraling around her. The feeling of being stretched gave way to a sense of floating, as though she were suspended in a void between realities. Gradually, the colors and patterns coalesced.

Arrival in the New World

When the disorienting transition finally ended, Wei found herself standing on solid ground in an entirely different environment. She was in a vast, open landscape that seemed to stretch infinitely in all directions. The sky above was a deep, twilight purple, dotted with unfamiliar constellations and two large moons that bathed the land in a soft, ethereal glow.

The ground beneath her was covered in strange, bioluminescent plants that pulsed with a gentle light, illuminating her path. Despite the alien surroundings, Wei felt an inexplicable sense of calm, as if the place itself was welcoming her.

The Alien Landscape

Exploring her surroundings, Wei marveled at the surreal beauty of the new world. Towering crystalline structures rose from the ground, refracting the moonlight into a spectrum of colors. Rivers of liquid light flowed through the landscape, their currents casting shimmering reflections on the bioluminescent flora.

She noticed signs of intelligent life — pathways carved into the crystal, strange symbols etched into the rocks, and artifacts that resembled tools and devices, albeit in forms and materials she couldn't immediately understand.

The Ancient City

Following one of the illuminated pathways, Wei arrived at an ancient city that seemed to blend seamlessly into the natural landscape. The architecture was unlike anything she had ever seen: buildings made of a translucent material that glowed softly from within, and structures that appeared to float above the ground.

As she ventured deeper into the city, she found a central plaza dominated by a massive, five-sided pyramid similar to the one on Mars. The realization struck her — this could be a sister pyramid, part of a network that spanned multiple worlds.

The Gateway Nexus

At the base of the pyramid, she discovered another gateway, surrounded by intricate carvings and symbols. The glyphs here were similar to those in the Martian pyramid, but more complex, suggesting a higher level of understanding or perhaps an older origin.

Examining the symbols, Wei realized that this gateway could connect to numerous other locations, possibly including Earth. Her heart raced with the possibility of returning home or discovering even more about the Martian civilization's reach across the cosmos.

The Guardian of Knowledge

As she pondered her next move, a shimmering figure emerged from the pyramid's entrance. It was a holographic projection of an alien being — tall and elegant, with elongated limbs and a serene, wise expression. The being spoke in a language that resonated in Wei's mind, not just as sound but as pure meaning.

"On behalf of the A'kara. Welcome, traveler," the guardian said. "You have accessed the Nexus of Worlds. Here, knowledge from countless civilizations is stored, preserved against the ravages of time. You seek understanding and a way home."

Wei nodded, her voice trembling with emotion. "Yes, I do. Can you help me? Can I return to Earth?"

The guardian's holographic eyes seemed to look deep into her soul. "The gateways connect many places. To return to your world, you must understand the paths and the sacrifices required. This knowledge is yours to seek, but you must prove yourself worthy."

The Trials of Worth

The guardian guided her into the pyramid, where she faced a series of trials in five chambers designed to test her intellect, courage, integrity, focus and knowledge. Each chamber presented her with challenges — complex puzzles, simulations of moral dilemmas, and physical tasks that pushed her to her limits. Wei stood at the entrance of the first chamber within the pyramid, her heart pounding with anticipation and a hint of trepidation. The guardian's words echoed in her mind:"To return to your world, you must prove yourself worthy."

It reminded her of the infamous chambers of the legendary Shaolin temple monks, who they had to pass for final examination. Although she practices traditional Chinese martial arts regularly for physical fitness, she is not as trained as a warrior monk. She took a deep breath and stepped forward, ready to face whatever challenges lay ahead.

The First Challenge: Chamber of Intellect

The first chamber was a vast hall filled with floating geometric shapes, each glowing with an inner light. Symbols and equations danced in the air, shifting and rearranging themselves in complex patterns.

Objective: Solve the geometric puzzles to unlock the next passage.

Wei recognized the symbols as a mix of Martian mathematics and spatial logic. She reached out to touch one of the floating shapes, and it responded by expanding into a three-dimensional puzzle. Each puzzle required her to manipulate the shapes and symbols into a harmonious configuration.

The First Puzzle: Rotating Tetrahedrons

The first puzzle involved aligning a series of rotating tetrahedrons (triangular pyramids) so that their shadows formed a specific pattern on the ground. Wei used her engineering skills to understand the mechanics of the rotations and quickly solved it.

The Second Puzzle: Balance of Energy Flows

The second puzzle required her to balance energy flows between interconnected shapes, akin to managing power grids. Drawing on her knowledge of electrical systems, she adjusted the flows until the shapes glowed in unison.

With each solved puzzle, a section of the wall dissolved, revealing a path to the next sub-chamber.

The Chamber of Intellect was a vast hall filled with floating geometric shapes, each glowing with an inner light. Symbols and equations danced in the air, shifting and rearranging themselves in complex patterns. The first two puzzles had tested the astronaut's spatial reasoning and engineering skills, but the third puzzle was even more challenging.

The Third Puzzle: Resonance of the Spheres

As the walls of the second puzzle chamber dissolved, revealing the path to the next chamber, Wei stepped forward, ready for whatever challenge lay ahead. The chamber was smaller than the previous ones, with a domed ceiling that sparkled with embedded crystals. In the center hovered a large spherical structure made up of smaller interconnected spheres, each emitting a unique tone.

Wei approached the structure, her keen eyes scanning the intricate network of spheres. Each smaller sphere contained symbols and waveforms etched into its surface, all pulsing with varying frequencies of light and sound.

Objective: Harmonize the frequencies of the spheres to unlock the next passage.

Initial Analysis

Wei recognized the challenge immediately. The symbols and waveforms were reminiscent of the puzzles she had solved earlier, but this time, the solution lay in her ability to understand and manipulate sound and light frequencies alone.

Wei said to herself:"These spheres... they represent different frequencies. Sound, light, maybe even electromagnetic waves. I need to synchronize them."

She reached out to touch one of the spheres, and it responded by emitting a clear tone that resonated through the chamber. The tone fluctuated, creating a ripple effect in the other spheres. She realized that each sphere's frequency affected the others.

Deciphering the Symbols

Wei began by examining the symbols on the nearest sphere. The hieroglyphs suggested a starting point: a fundamental frequency that needed to be established first. She adjusted the controls on a nearby panel, tuning the sphere to match the indicated frequency.

Step 1: Establish the Fundamental Frequency

As she fine-tuned the first sphere, it emitted a steady, harmonious tone. The surrounding spheres responded, their light and sound frequencies beginning to align with the fundamental frequency.

Wei affirmed:"Alright, one down. Now to adjust the others."

Balancing the Frequencies

Each subsequent sphere required precise adjustments. Wei used her knowledge of acoustics and electromagnetic waves to balance the frequencies, ensuring that each sphere resonated in harmony with the fundamental tone.

Step 2: Synchronize the Secondary Frequencies

Wei moved from sphere to sphere, her fingers deftly manipulating the controls. She adjusted the wavelengths and amplitudes, bringing each sphere into alignment. As she did so, the chamber filled with a harmonious blend of light and sound, creating a resonant symphony that echoed through the domed ceiling.

Tuning the Final Sphere

The final sphere was the most complex. It contained multiple overlapping waveforms, each representing a different type of frequency. Wei understood that this sphere was the keystone of the puzzle, and its alignment would complete the harmonic structure.

Step 3: Harmonize the Overlapping Frequencies

Wei took a deep breath, focusing her mind. She visualized the waveforms, each layer representing a different element of the A'kara technology. Using her expertise, she adjusted the frequencies one by one, ensuring that they meshed perfectly with the existing harmonic structure.

As the final adjustments fell into place, the sphere emitted a clear, pure tone that resonated through the entire chamber. The other spheres responded in kind, their lights and sounds merging into a cohesive, harmonious whole.

The Passage Opens

With the final puzzle solved, the chamber vibrated with a gentle hum. The spherical structure began to glow brighter, and the symbols on its surface illuminated the room with a soft, ethereal light. The walls shimmered and slowly dissolved, revealing a hidden passage.

Wei:"I did it. The frequencies are harmonized."

She stepped back, admiring her work. The sense of accomplishment filled her with pride, knowing that she had solved the puzzle through her intellect and skill.

As she moved forward through the newly revealed passage, the echoes of the harmonious symphony lingered in the chamber behind her. Wei knew that her journey was far from over, and the mysteries of the A'kara civilization continued to unfold before her. She was ready to face whatever challenges lay ahead, armed with the knowledge and determination that had brought her this far.

The Second Challenge: Chamber of Courage

The second chamber was an expansive, dimly lit arena with an eerie silence. Shadows moved at the edges of her vision.

Objective: Face and overcome physical and psychological fears.

Suddenly, the shadows coalesced into tangible forms — creatures that embodied her deepest fears and insecurities. They lunged at her with terrifying speed, forcing her to react instinctively.

Wei's heart raced as she evaded the creatures. She realized that physical prowess alone wouldn't suffice; she had to confront her fears head-on. Drawing from her martial arts training, she centered herself, focusing her mind and controlling her breathing.

She faced each creature, acknowledging the fear it represented. As she did, the creatures began to dissolve, their menace fading. The last creature was a representation of her fear of failure, towering and imposing. Summoning all her courage, she stepped forward, confronting it with the conviction of her successes and the lessons from her failures. The creature dissipated into a fine mist, and the path to the next chamber opened.

The Third Challenge: Chamber of Integrity

The third chamber was a serene garden with a tranquil pool at ist center. Around the pool were statues of Martian beings in various poses of meditation.

Objective: Make ethical decisions that demonstrate integrity and compassion.

Wei approached the pool and saw her reflection, alongside holograms of her crewmates and loved ones. The guardian's voice echoed around her:"To proceed, you must make decisions that balance logic with empathy."

Holographic scenarios began to unfold around her, each presenting a moral dilemma:

Resource Allocation: A settlement needed critical supplies to survive, but distributing them fairly would mean that everyone got just enough, while favoring one group could ensure their long-term survival but at the cost of the others. Wei chose to distribute the supplies fairly, ensuring that everyone had a chance, reflecting her belief in equality and fairness.

Sacrifice for the Greater Good: A scenario depicted a crisis where one individual needed to sacrifice themselves to save many others. The individual was a friend. Wei faced the emotional turmoil of making a decision that valued the greater good over personal attachment. She chose to save the many, understanding the painful but necessary logic behind it.

Forgiveness and Redemption: A scenario where a former adversary sought redemption and help in a dire situation. Wei had to decide whether to trust them. Drawing from her experiences of teamwork and the potential for change, she chose to offer help, demonstrating her belief in second chances and the capacity for growth.

Each decision she made was weighed by the guardian, and with each correct moral choice, the garden around her bloomed brighter and more vibrant. Finally, a path of illuminated stones led her to the penultimate chamber.

The Forth Challenge: Chamber of Focus

The moment Wei crossed the threshold, she entered a large, dimly lit chamber. A cool, eerie wind brushed against her skin, carrying with it the scent of ancient stone and something indefinably alien. The walls were decorated with intricate carvings and symbols that glowed faintly and cast ghostly shadows.

Objective: Maintain mental fortitude, precision, adaptability, and physical discipline.

At the center of the room stood a pedestal made of a material that shimmered like liquid silver. Resting upon it was a bow, unlike any she had ever seen. The bow seemed to pulse with a faint inner light, and beside it lay a quiver of arrows, each tipped with a glowing point.

Wei approached the pedestal cautiously. As she reached out to take the bow, a deep, resonant voice filled the chamber, speaking in a language that she somehow understood:"Prove your worth through concentration and skill. Only then shall you pass."

With the bow now in her hands, Wei felt a strange connection to it, as if it were an extension of herself. She slung the quiver over her shoulder and took a few steps back, scanning the chamber for the first sign of a challenge.

Without warning, a series of targets appeared along the walls and across the floor. Each target bore a different symbol and glowed with varying intensities. Some were stationary, while others began to move, darting erratically through the air or sliding swiftly along the ground.

Wei nocked an arrow, her senses sharpening as she focused on the nearest target. She drew the bowstring back, feeling the perfect tension, and released. The arrow flew true, striking the center of the target with a satisfying thud. Instantly, the target vanished, and another appeared further away.

As she hit each target, they disappeared only to be replaced by new ones, each presenting a more complex challenge. Targets began to appear in quick succession, moving faster and more unpredictably. The air filled with distracting noises — echoes, whispers, and the distant rumble of unseen machinery — all designed to break her concentration.

Wei's training and natural aptitude for archery came to the fore. She blocked out the distractions, narrowing her focus to a razor-sharp edge. She breathed steadily, each exhale releasing tension and sharpening her aim. Her movements were fluid and precise, a dance of focus and skill.

Halfway through the trial, the environment shifted. Columns rose from the floor, obstructing her line of sight and providing cover for the moving targets. Some targets were now partially obscured, requiring her to adjust her aim and timing.

Sweat trickled down her forehead as she drew, aimed, and released in a seamless flow. She moved swiftly to find better vantage points, her mind and body in perfect harmony. She hit target after target, her confidence growing with each successful shot.

Suddenly, the chamber's lighting changed, and the final challenge presented itself: a small, fast-moving orb that darted around the room with incredible speed. It emitted a high-pitched hum, making it even harder to track. This was the ultimate test of her concentration and skill.

Wei took a deep breath, calming her racing heart. She tracked the orb's movement, anticipating its erratic path. She nocked her final arrow, drew the bowstring back, and waited for the perfect moment. Time seemed to slow as she focused entirely on the target.

With a sudden release, the arrow shot forward with deadly precision. It struck the orb dead center, shattering it into a burst of light. The chamber fell silent, and the glowing symbols on the walls brightened, illuminating the entire space.

The resonant voice returned, this time with a tone of respect and approval:"You have proven your worth. The path is open."

The far wall of the chamber slid open, revealing a passageway leading to the final chamber. Wei, still holding the bow and quiver, felt a surge of triumph and relief.

Wei smiled, though her muscles ached and her mind was still reeling from the intensity of the trial. Although this trail had been tailored to her, it was the hardest thing she had ever done. But she couldn't have done it if she hadn't known that somewhere out there her teammates were waiting for her to give them a sign of life.

The Fifth Challenge: Chamber of Knowledge

The final chamber was a grand library, its walls lined with shelves of crystalline tablets and holographic scrolls. At its center stood a pedestal with a complex control panel.

Objective: Unlock and understand the ultimate knowledge of the Martian civilization.

Wei approached the control panel, which displayed intricate patterns and alien scripts. She had to decipher the language and input the correct sequences to access the Martians' most guarded secrets. Using the knowledge she had accumulated and her skills in linguistics and cryptography, she began to translate the symbols.

Each correct translation activated a part of the pedestal, revealing more of the Martians' advanced technologies and philosophies. The process was painstaking, requiring intense concentration and a deep understanding of the context and subtleties of the Martian language.

After almost hours of work, the final piece fell into place, and the pedestal glowed with a bright, pulsating light. A holographic projection of the Martian guardian appeared once more, nodding approvingly.

"You have demonstrated intellect, courage, integrity, and the capacity to understand and respect our knowledge. You are now worthy of the gateway's secrets."

The Revelation and Return

With the trials complete, the guardian presented Wei with a detailed map of the gateway network and instructions on how to navigate it. Among the destinations, she found the coordinates for Earth.

Activating the gateway, Wei once again felt the disorienting pull of space-time. When the sensation subsided, she found herself in an ancient chamber beneath the sands of Egypt, surrounded by familiar hieroglyphs and the warm glow of sunlight filtering through a narrow opening.

She stepped out into the Egyptian desert, her mind brimming with the knowledge and experiences she had gained. She knew that the secrets she carried from the Martian civilization would shape the future of humanity.

As she stood beneath the vast, star-filled sky, Wei felt a profound connection to the cosmos — a bridge between worlds, forged through trials that tested the very essence of her being. She had returned, not just as an astronaut, but as a bearer of ancient wisdom and a beacon of hope for all mankind.

Chapter 16: Reestablishing Contact

Wei's mind racing with thoughts of her crewmates still on Mars. She needed to reestablish contact to inform them of her survival, the successful completion of her trials, and the crucial knowledge she now possessed. The gateway had returned her to Earth, but her mission was far from over.

Finding Communication Tools

First, Wei had to find a means of communication. She went back inside the pyramid. It was ancient, but there were signs of Martian influence. She hoped that the ancient Egyptians had left behind tools or knowledge that could aid her.

As she explored the pyramid's chambers, she discovered a hidden room filled with artifacts that hinted at advanced technology. Among the relics was a device that resembled an ancient form of a communicator, its design remarkably sophisticated despite its age.

Wei carefully examined the device, noting its similarities to Martian technology. It appeared to be a type of transceiver, possibly capable of long-range communication. She worked quickly, using her engineering skills to reactivate the dormant device. She adjusted its settings, aligning it with the frequencies she had learned from the Martian gateway.

With the communicator operational, Wei needed to establish a clear link to Mars. The device hummed to life, its intricate circuitry glowing with an otherworldly light. She calibrated the transceiver, adjusting for the vast distance between Earth and Mars and the delay caused by the speed of light.

"Come on, come on," she muttered to herself, her fingers flying over the controls. She sent out a series of pulses, encoded with a message and her coordinates, hoping to catch the attention of her crewmates.

As she waited for a response, Wei felt a pang of anxiety. What if the message didn't reach them? What if the device wasn't powerful enough? She paced the chamber, glancing frequently at the communicator, willing it to succeed.

After what felt like an eternity, the device emitted a series of beeps, signaling an incoming transmission. Her heart leaped with hope.

Contact Reestablished

The communicator crackled to life, and she heard Commander Harris's voice, faint but unmistakable. "Wei? Is that you? This is Mars base. Do you copy?"

Tears of relief welled in her eyes. "Yes, it's me! I'm on Earth, in Egypt. I found another gateway. I'm safe."

The line was silent for a moment, and then Commander Harris's voice came through, filled with emotion. "Thank God. We thought we lost you. Are you okay? What happened?"

What was special about this new form of communication compared to previous terrestrial communication was that it now worked in real time without the average one-way communication delay of 12.5

minutes. Wei quickly summarized her journey, explaining the trials she had faced and the knowledge she had gained about the Martian civilization called A'kara. She detailed the existence of the gateway network and its potential to connect multiple worlds, including a direct link back to Earth.

As she spoke, the other crew members joined the transmission. Ivan's voice was filled with a mix of relief and guilt. "Wei, I... I'm so sorry. We had no idea what would happen."

"It's okay, Ivan," she replied, her voice steady. "What's important now is what we do next. I have information that could change everything. The Martian knowledge, their technology — it's incredible. We need to study it and understand it fully."

Emily, getting straight to the point as a scientist, asked:"Can you transmit the data back to us? We need to analyze it and see how it can help us here on Mars."

Wei adjusted the communicator, connecting it to her portable data pad. She began transmitting the encoded data she had gathered during her trials. "I'm sending everything now. It might take a while due to the distance, but you should start receiving it soon."

As the data transmission commenced, the team discussed their next steps. Commander Harris took charge, coordinating the efforts between Earth and Mars.

"We need to secure the pyramid here and protect the gateway," Wei suggested. "If others find it without understanding its significance, it could be dangerous."

"Agreed," Commander Harris replied. "We'll continue our work here and prepare for potential travel through the gateways. This could be a turning point for humanity."

Klaus butted in:"I envy you a bit, now you have a chance to enjoy a seaside resort with beach, drinks and palm trees!"

Wei replied:"Sure, but tempus fugit. Even back down here I won't have much time left, I will be very busy with securing the pyramid and being the full-time advisor at mission control. But once we all have the reunion, I promise that I will keep you a cool beer reserved, Klaus."

Then Sophie interjected:"Wei, I don't know how to say, but I am sorry really."

Wei retorted:"Don't mention it. Let's bury what happened. I forgive you. As a matter of fact, thanks to you I had the chance of a lifetime to have this peculiar experience to go where no woman has gone before."

Ivan's voice, still tinged with emotion, cut through. "Wei, we're proud of you. Your courage and perseverance have given us a chance to achieve something extraordinary."

"Thank you, Ivan," she responded, feeling the weight of their shared mission.

"Let's make sure we honor Wei's sacrifice and the legacy of the Martian civilization", Commander Harris decided.

As the transmission ended, Wei felt a profound sense of accomplishment and purpose. She had bridged the gap between worlds, not just physically but intellectually and emotionally. The knowledge she carried was a beacon for humanity's future, a testament to the enduring spirit of exploration and discovery. She left the pyramid and looked out over the vast desert. She left the pyramid and looked out at the vast desert.

The sun setting over the horizon, casting long shadows over the ancient sands.

As the stars began to twinkle in the night sky, Wei felt a deep connection to the universe. The gateways had shown her that distances

could be bridged, knowledge could be shared, and despite the vastness of space, unity was possible.

After this exciting adventure, Wei was totatally exhausted. So she was
overcome by tiredness and fell asleep on the spot on a sand hill next
to the Egyptian pyramid.

Chapter 17: The A'kara Civilization

Unveiling the A'kara History

The journey into the depths of the Martian pyramid was both a physical and intellectual odyssey. As the astronauts explored the intricate passages and chambers, they uncovered the rich tapestry of the A'kara civilization's history, piecing together the story of a people whose achievements and understanding of the universe were far beyond anything humanity had ever imagined.

One of the chambers of the pyramid held the key to understanding the A'kara. The walls were adorned with detailed carvings and hiero- glyphs, each one a fragment of the A'kara's epic story. In the center of the room stood a large, intricately designed pedestal, upon which rested a crystalline tablet. This tablet, when activated, projected holo- graphic images and narrated the history of the A'kara in their own melodious language.

As the astronauts activated the tablet, the room came alive with light. Holographic figures, shimmering with an ethereal glow, moved across the chamber, reenacting scenes from the A'kara's history. The- se projections, coupled with the hieroglyphs, created a vivid and im- mersive experience.

The projection began with the early days of the A'kara. They were shown as a flourishing society, their cities filled with towering struc- tures and advanced technology. The A'kara had harnessed the power of Martian resources, mastering energy sources that were clean, limit- less, and sustainable. They lived in harmony with their environment, their society marked by a deep respect for both the planet and the cosmos.

The next phase depicted the A'kara's insatiable curiosity about the universe. They built observatories and space vessels, exploring the solar system and beyond. Their scientists and philosophers delved into the mysteries of life, energy, and consciousness. This era was marked by groundbreaking discoveries and the development of tech- nologies that allowed them to manipulate energy and matter at a fun- damental level.

As their understanding of the universe grew, the A'kara realized their role as cosmic stewards. The holograms showed the formation of the

Celestial Council, a group of enlightened beings who guided the A'kara in their quest to maintain cosmic balance. The A'kara learned to channel cosmic energies, using them to sustain their society and protect their world from external threats.

The most profound chapter of their history focused on the A'kara's quest for immortality. The projections illustrated their experiments with consciousness and energy, seeking to transcend their physical forms. They discovered that by merging their essence with certain resonant materials, such as the stones of the pyramid, they could achieve a state of eternal existence.

The A'kara's concept of immortality was not just about living forever; it was about transcending the limitations of physical existence and becoming part of the cosmic tapestry.

The astronauts learned that the A'kara had developed intricate rituals to prepare for transcendence. These rituals involved aligning one's energy with the cosmic rhythms and undergoing a series of mental and spiritual preparations. The final step was the merging of one's consciousness with a resonant material, effectively becoming a part of the pyramid and the cosmic energy field.

Upon transcending, the A'kara's individual identities dissolved, and they became part of a collective consciousness. This collective entity was vast and interconnected, allowing the A'kara to experience the universe in ways unimaginable to physical beings. They could perceive cosmic events, influence energy flows, and maintain the balance of the universe.

The A'kara's immortality came with a profound sense of responsibility. As eternal guardians, they were tasked with protecting the universe from entropy and chaos. Their consciousness, dispersed like stardust, played a crucial role in sustaining the fabric of existence. This role was not just a duty but a harmonious existence, where they found purpose and fulfillment in their guardianship.

As the holographic narration ended, the astronauts stood in silent awe, absorbing the magnitude of what they had just witnessed.

Commander Harris started to comment:"This is beyond anything we could have imagined. The A'kara weren't just advanced — they had a wisdom that transcended our understanding of life and the universe. Their understanding of cosmic energies and their role as stewards of reality is incredible."

Emily followed to speak:"These hieroglyphs are more than just a record of their achievements. They tell a story of a civilization that transcended physical existence. The way they merged with the pyramid to achieve immortality is both fascinating and terrifying. Their pursuit of immortality wasn't about escaping death but about becoming one with the cosmos. Their consciousness became part of the universe's fabric, maintaining its balance. It's a beautiful and humbling concept."

After that Ivan found his words:"And their sense of responsibility... They didn't seek power or control but harmony and protection. Their legacy is a testament to the potential of intelligent life when it pursues knowledge and understanding. Moreover, they sacrificed their individuality for the greater good, becoming part of a collective consciousness. It's a level of selflessness that's hard to comprehend. But it also raises questions about the nature of identity and consciousness."

After Wei's sign of life, Sophie was fully rehabilitated in the team, although a certain mistrust remained within in the team. She said:"The new constellation in the sky — it's a beautiful reminder of their sacrifice and our connection to the cosmos. We're not just explorers; we're part of something much bigger. We have so much to learn from them. Their technologies, their philosophies, their understanding of energy and consciousness — it's a treasure trove of knowledge."

Emily added:"And their story isn't just about the past. It's a guide for us, a roadmap to a higher purpose. We have a duty to honor their legacy and use what we've learned to protect and enhance our world."

Klaus, who has been silent during that time. His thoughts still wandered to Wei and the traumatic event, although he had to admit that the classic realization soon set in: out of sight, out of mind, because in front of him stood Emily in all her glory, whom he could see and hear, but would soon also be able to experience with all other senses, with smell, taste and touch… However, this had to wait until they had reached the habitat. He suddenly fell in for her and he sensed that she sensed it too. After a short break Klaus was obliged to comment:"Their hieroglyphs and the holographic records — they're not just historical artifacts. They're messages, teachings meant to guide us. We need to decode every bit of information we can and share it with the world. The A'kara's understanding of cosmic rhythms and their role as guardians offers us a new perspective on our own existence. We have much to learn from them, and much to strive for."

With a renewed sense of purpose, the astronauts began documenting their findings in meticulous detail. They knew that their discoveries could change the course of human history, offering insights into not only advanced technologies but also the profound philosophical and ethical teachings of the A'kara.

They established a secure communication link with Earth, transmitting the wealth of knowledge they had uncovered. They also reported about Wei's whereabouts and her adventure. They gave through the exact coordinates to pick her up to bring her over to mission control. Although she was about 225 million kilometers (140 million miles) away, she was now the most valuable, indispensible asset on Earth for them.

Their mission had evolved from exploration to preservation and education. They were now the custodians of the A'kara's legacy, charged with the task of ensuring that humanity learned from the wisdom of this ancient Martian civilization.

As they prepared for the next phase of their mission, the astronauts felt a deep connection to the A'kara, a kinship that transcended time and space. They were part of a cosmic continuum, bound by the shared pursuit of knowledge and the eternal quest to understand the mysteries of the universe.

Chapter 18: The Hidden Chamber

The Martian pyramid loomed above the astronauts, casting long shadows across the red sands of the planet's surface. The discovery of new chambers within the ancient structure had become routine for the team, yet each new find filled them with a mix of excitement and trepidation. Today, however, would be different.

Emily, using her geological expertise, had been examining the pyramid's outer structure for any anomalies. Her keen eye for detail soon paid off when she noticed a slight irregularity in the stonework on the north side. Gathering the rest of the team, they began to investigate.

Emily pointed to the wall:"Look here. The stones are different in this section. They might be concealing something."

Klaus examined the stones:"You're right. There are fine seams here, almost like a hidden door. Let's see if we can open it."

With careful precision, they traced the seams and pressed on the stones in various patterns. After several attempts, the stones began to move, sliding away to reveal a narrow passage leading deeper into the pyramid. The astronauts exchanged excited glances before stepping inside, their flashlights cutting through the darkness.

The passage was long and winding, the walls adorned with more hieroglyphs and carvings. Finally, they reached a large, circular chamber. In the center of the chamber stood a pedestal with three objects resting on it, each bathed in a soft, ethereal glow.

The First Artifact

Sophie wide-eyed:"What do you think these are?"

Commander Harris stepped closer:"They look like some kind of advanced tools or weapons. Let's examine them carefully."

The first object was a sleek, scepter-like device made of an unknown metal that gleamed under their lights. It was engraved with intricate designs and had three distinct settings marked by symbols.

Ivan examined the scepter and said:"This looks like a weapon. Maybe it has different modes. Let's see... these symbols might indicate the settings."

Klaus pointed to the discreetly concealed symbols:"This one resembles a stun symbol. And here, a flame. The last one, a skull. Stunning, burning, and killing."

Commander Harris nodded:"We'll have to test it to be sure, but it seems plausible. We should handle it with extreme care."

Ivan volunteered:"Go ahead, Klaus. Give me a dose with the stun setting please. If I won't spring to life, give me this epinephrine shot."

Sophie curiously asked:"Epinephrine?"

Ivan replied:"Yes, this is synthetic adrenaline, and may help to..."

Commander Harris interrupted:"Out of the question. If you as our medical doctor won't recover, we will have big trouble."

Klaus stepped forward:"I'll take it."

Suddenly Emily pushed Klaus aside:"We women are also strong and are not part of the weaker sex. I insist on being the test subject."

Commander Harris was convinced and gave a green light. In military command style, he said only briefly:"Permission granted!"

Without hesitation, Ivan pointed the scepter to Emily and pushed the stun button. Emily fainted immediately and Klaus caught her before falling to the ground.

After about 30 seconds Ivan approached to Emily and gave a revitalization shot.

Emily felt dizzy and murmured:"Where am I? What happened?"

Ivan explained:"This is normal. Coming out of anesthesia you will often experience retrograde amnesia."

Emily gradually recovered and got up on her feet again. She smiled gratefully at Klaus, who had held her carefully in his arms the whole time. She knew herself that it was a primal instinct to be protected that came up in her. But she enjoyed it so much and somehow she also sensed that Klaus enjoyed his role just as much.

The Second Artifact

Next to the scepter was a slender rod, not unlike a modern medical scanner, but with a smooth, organic design. It emitted a soft, green light and had a pin at the end. The device seemed not only to be functional but also a piece of art, designed with meticulous attention to detail and an understanding of both aesthetics and ergonomics. It was crafted from a smooth, iridescent material that reflected a spectrum of colors depending on the angle of the light. The material had the durability of metal but the warmth and subtle flexibility of a fine polymer, suggesting a composite material of advanced design. The surface of the rod was adorned with intricate, flowing patterns that seemed to shift and change as one moved around it. These patterns were not merely decorative; they contained micro-etchings of symbols and glyphs that were believed to be part of the device's control and activation systems. The engravings were delicate and precise, hinting at the use of advanced laser etching or a similar technology. At one end of the rod was a small, round crystal embedded into the surface. This crystal emitted a soft, green light when the rod was in use. Surrounding the crystal were concentric rings of minute, luminescent symbols that glowed faintly. To activate the rod, the user needed to press the crystal and rotate the rings to align specific symbols, which likely used the rod for different medical functions.

Emily picking up the rod:"This looks like it could be a medical tool. See how it's shaped? It's designed to be held and directed easily."

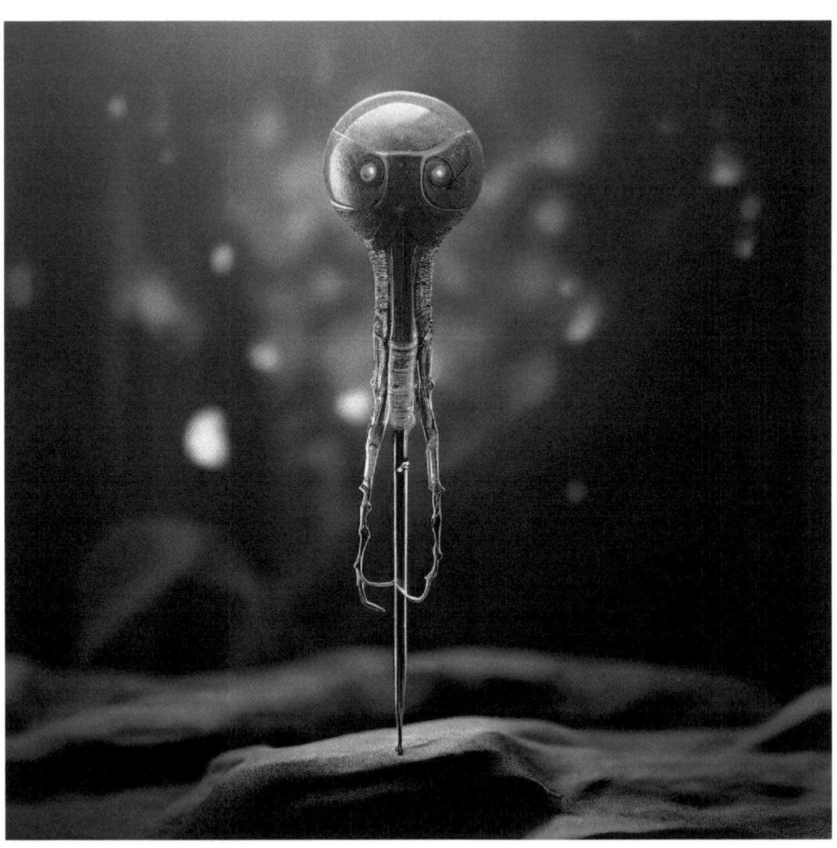

Sophie activated the device:"Let's test it. Ivan, do you have any minor wounds?"

Ivan showed a small cut on his arm:"Here. Be gentle."

Sophie directed the green light over Ivan's wound.

Ivan's face contorted in pain and he groaned:"Ouch! Be careful, I am human."

Almost instantly, the cut began to close, the skin knitting back together seamlessly.

Ivan was astonished and enthusiastically said:"It's a medical device! Incredible. This could revolutionize emergency care."

Ivan grabbed the medical rod from Sophie and put it carefully in his bag. He was convinced that this tool could be used more often on this mission.

The Third Artifact

Finally, they turned their attention to the third object, a small, intricate piece of technology that resembled a bracelet. The bracelet was composed of a lustrous, unknown alloy that reflected light in a way that seemed almost liquid. It had a seamless, fluid appearance, with no visible joints or seams, indicating an advanced level of metallurgical expertise. The bracelet was slightly larger than a typical wristband, designed to fit comfortably around the wrist without being cumbersome. Encircling the outer surface of the bracelet were delicate engravings that resembled a fusion of geometric patterns and organic motifs. These patterns interwove in a continuous loop, creating a mesmerizing visual effect. Embedded within the engravings were tiny, glowing symbols that pulsed with a faint, ethereal light. These symbols were reminiscent of the hieroglyphs found on the pyramid walls, suggesting that they held significant meaning or function related to the device's operation. At the center of the bracelet was a small, raised crystal, about the size of a pea. This crystal emitted a soft, multicolored glow that seemed to shift and change as it was observed from different angles. The astronauts surmised that this crystal was the key to activating the device. As Klaus touched it, he shimmered and disappeared from view.

Emily gasped:"Klaus, where did you go?"

Suddenly Emily was touched by invisible hands from behind.

Emily giggled with delight and replied energetically:"Naughty boy. Please behave yourself, Klaus. We have spectators here!"

Klaus reappeared:"It's a cloaking device! I was completely invisible. This could be extremely useful for exploration and protection."

And Emily flirted to Klaus: "And for seduction!"

As they continued to search the area, the astronauts discovered more bracelets in a kind of trunk. This meant that each member of the team was now well equipped with a personal camouflage cap.

Commander Harris said in a serious voice:"We need to document these findings and integrate them into our mission. These tools are advanced beyond anything we have, and they could be crucial for our survival and success here on Mars."

Gathering the new devices, the astronauts made their way back to their base camp. The discovery of the scepter, medical stick, and cloaking device added a new dimension to their mission. They were now equipped with technology that could protect them, heal them, and render them invisible if needed. The implications were vast, and they knew they had to use these tools wisely.

As they sat around their camp, discussing the potential uses and consequences of their new discoveries, a sense of determination settled over the group. They were not just explorers; they were pioneers standing at the threshold of a new era of human discovery.

Commander Harris said resolutely: "We've found incredible tools here, but we need to stay focused. Our mission is to uncover the secrets of this civilization and learn from them. Let's use these tools to aid us, but let's not forget why we're here."

The team nodded in agreement, each member understanding the gravity of their situation. With the new discoveries in hand, they felt more prepared for whatever lay ahead. The mysteries of the Martian pyramid were far from fully unraveled, but with each step, they were closer to understanding the ancient A'kara and their incredible legacy.

Chapter 19: The Celestial Council

The astronauts ventured deeper into the Martian pyramid, their path illuminated by the soft, pulsating glow of the hieroglyphs. They had unraveled puzzles that tested their intellect and unity, each step bringing them closer to the heart of the A'kara civilization. As they entered the next chamber, an overwhelming sense of anticipation filled the air.

The Grand Chamber

The chamber was vast, its domed ceiling adorned with constellations that sparkled like the night sky. The walls were lined with intricate carvings depicting the A'kara's history and achievements.

A monstrous figure with nine fingers on each hand was enthroned in the center of the room surrounded by six tall, ethereal figures made of shimmering light and energy.

Commander Harris took a step forward, his eyes wide with wonder. "What is this place?"

Emily studied the carvings on the walls. "These must be the Celestial Council, the guardians of the A'kara's knowledge and legacy."

The figures seemed to acknowledge their presence, their forms glowing brighter. A gentle hum filled the chamber, resonating with an otherworldly energy. The astronauts instinctively knew they were in the presence of beings far beyond their understanding.

The First Encounter

One of the figures stepped forward, its form becoming more defined. It had a humanoid shape but radiated a profound energy that transcended physicality. When it spoke, its voice was a harmonious blend of tones, resonating directly in the minds of the astronauts.

The Celestial Being began:"Welcome, travelers from Earth. We are the Celestial Council, stewards of the A'kara civilization. You have proven your intellect and unity by overcoming the trials set before you."

Sophie felt a shiver run down her spine. "Who were the A'kara? What happened to them?"

The figure's glow intensified, and images began to form in the air around them, illustrating the rise and fall of the A'kara civilization.

Rise of the A'kara

The A'kara were an ancient and highly advanced civilization that flourished on Mars eons ago. They had mastered the use of cosmic energies, harnessing the power of stars and planets to fuel their technology and sustain their society. The A'kara civilization was at its zenith, a beacon of advanced technology and enlightened philosophy. Their cities were wonders of engineering, seamlessly integrated into the Martian landscape. Towers of crystal and metal reached toward the sky, powered by a combination of solar and geothermal energy. The A'kara had mastered sustainable living, ensuring that their planet thrived alongside their technological advancements.

The Celestial Being explained:"We were once like you, explorers and innovators, seeking to understand the mysteries of the universe. Our knowledge grew vast, our achievements great."

The images showed the A'kara engaging in various scientific and cultural pursuits. They studied the stars, delved into the secrets of the atom, and created art and music.

The A'kara had a profound understanding of the universe's cosmic rhythms. They established a network of knowledge and energy, extending their influence to other planets and even different dimensions. Their ultimate goal was to maintain balance and harmony across the cosmos.

The Approach of Entropy

Despite their successes, the A'kara could not escape the fundamental laws of the universe. They began to detect subtle changes in their environment — shifts in the magnetic field, fluctuations in the planet's core temperature, and anomalies in the cosmic radiation they received.

Klaus commented:"They were witnessing the signs of planetary decay."

The Celestial Being nodded. "Indeed. Our scientists predicted that Mars was slowly succumbing to entropy. The core was cooling, the atmosphere thinning, and the natural resources dwindling. We had to act to preserve our legacy."

The astronauts watched in rapt attention, their minds absorbing the profound tale of a civilization's struggle against cosmic inevitability.

The Catastrophic Event

The tipping point came when a series of massive asteroid impacts bombarded Mars, stripping away significant portions of its already fragile atmosphere. The resulting storms wreaked havoc on the planet's surface, causing widespread devastation.

Commander Harris presumed:"This seems to prove the controversial Titius-Bode Law with the missing planet, which also dragged Mars into the abyss due to its destruction by asteroid impacts."

The Celestial Being explained:"The asteroid impacts were a wake-up call. We realized that our time as physical beings was limited. We had to find a way to preserve our knowledge and essence before it was too late."

The images showed the A'kara scrambling to protect their cities, their scientists working tirelessly to develop a solution. It was a race against time, as the planet's condition worsened with each passing sol.

The Plan for Transcendence

The A'kara's greatest minds conceived a bold plan: to transcend their physical forms and merge their consciousness with the fabric of the pyramid, a structure that could withstand the ravages of time and cosmic forces. This pyramid would serve as a repository for their collective knowledge and essence, ensuring their legacy would endure.

The Celestial Being reported:"We constructed the pyramid using materials that could endure for eons. It became our ark, a vessel to carry our consciousness and knowledge into the future."

The images depicted the construction of the pyramid, a monumental effort involving the entire civilization. The structure was designed to harness and store cosmic energies, creating a stable environment for their consciousness to reside.

The Great Transition Ceremony

The culmination of their efforts was the Great Transition Ceremony. The entire population gathered around the pyramid, their faces filled with a mix of hope and solemn determination. The leaders of the A'kara, including the future members of the Celestial Council, stood at the forefront, ready to lead their people into a new existence.

The Celestial Being explained:"The ceremony was a profound moment in our history. We used our technology to convert our physical forms into pure energy, merging our consciousness with the pyramid."

The images showed a breathtaking spectacle of light and energy. The A'kara stood in concentric circles around the pyramid, their bodies dissolving into shimmering streams of energy that flowed into the structure. The pyramid absorbed the energy, its walls glowing with an inner light as the consciousness of an entire civilization merged into one.

The Emergence of the Celestial Council

As the last of the A'kara joined the collective consciousness within the pyramid, the Celestial Council emerged. These beings of pure energy embodied the wisdom and knowledge of the A'kara, tasked with guarding the pyramid and its secrets for eternity.

The Celestial Being reported:"We became the Celestial Council, stewards of our civilization's legacy. Our purpose is to guide and protect, to ensure that our knowledge serves the greater good of the cosmos."

The Legacy of Immortality

Emily gazed at the figures, awe-struck. "They achieved a form of immortality by becoming one with the pyramid."

The Celestial Being nodded. "Indeed. By transcending their physical forms, the A'kara ensured their legacy would endure. Their consciousness became part of the pyramid, their wisdom preserved for those who would come after."

Klaus asked, "What was the purpose of the trials we've faced?"

The Celestial Being answered:"The trials were designed to test your intellect, unity, and integrity. Only those who possess these qualities are deemed worthy of accessing the full knowledge and power of the A'kara. You have proven yourselves capable."

The Cosmic Key

The chamber filled with a brilliant light, and the figures of the Celestial Council began to merge, forming a single, radiant entity. This being extended a hand, and a stream of energy flowed from it, creating floating holographic images of symbols, equations, and star maps inside a key.

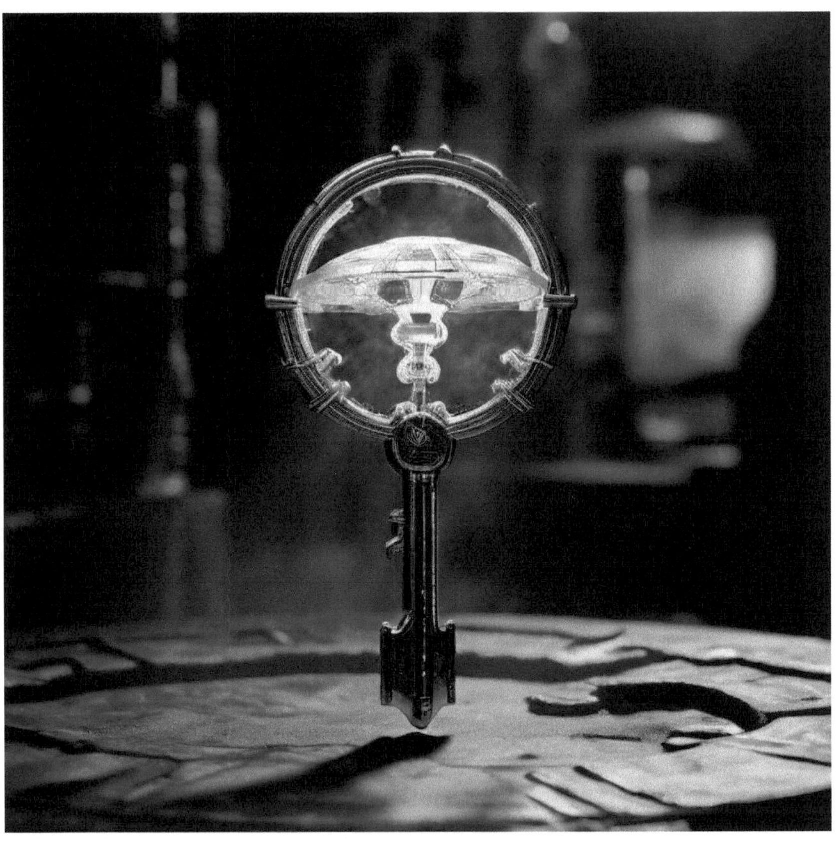

The Celestial Being clarified:"This is the Cosmic Key, the culmination of the A'kara's knowledge. It holds secrets of the universe, advanced technologies, and it is the key to achieving harmony and balance in your own world."

Ivan stepped closer, captivated by the swirling images. "This could change everything for humanity."

Sophie agreed. "It's a gift beyond measure. But why share it with us?"

The Celestial Being replied:"The A'kara believed in the potential of other civilizations to contribute to the cosmic order. By sharing this knowledge, we hope to guide you towards a future of enlightenment and balance."

The images faded, leaving the astronauts standing in the chamber, their minds reeling from the magnitude of what they had witnessed. Commander Harris stepped forward to grab the Cosmic Key that was floating in front of them.

Reflections and Resolutions

Emily looked at her team, determination shining in her eyes. "They sacrificed their physical existence to preserve their essence. It's both awe-inspiring and humbling."

As he gestured with the key in his hand, Commander Harris added: "And they entrusted us with their legacy with this key. We have a responsibility to honor that trust. We accept this knowledge with gratitude and humility. We will use it to better our world and ensure it's shared wisely."

Klaus concluded:"We've been given a rare opportunity. Let's honor the knowledge of the A'kara by ensuring we make the most of it. It's a gift, but also a burden."

The Celestial Being's light dimmed slightly, signifying a moment of solemnity. "Remember, with great knowledge comes great responsibility. Use it to foster peace and understanding, and to protect the balance of your world and the cosmos."

The team stood in silence, each of them reflecting on the weight of the knowledge they had been given. The story of the A'kara's transcendence was a testament to the power of unity, intellect, and the will to endure. Armed with this understanding and with the Cosmic Key, they felt a renewed sense of purpose as they prepared to venture further into the pyramid, ready to unlock more secrets and carry the legacy of the A'kara forward.

Chapter 20: The Time Machine Gate

The Discovery

The Martian pyramid, with its imposing five-sided structure and intricate carvings, had already revealed many secrets to the astronauts. Each chamber they explored seemed to unlock a new piece of the ancient A'kara civilization's legacy. Yet, they had a feeling that the greatest discovery was still hidden somewhere within its labyrinthine halls.

After sols of exploration and deciphering hieroglyphs, the team reached the central chamber, a vast, circular room that seemed to be the heart of the pyramid. The walls were adorned with symbols and glyphs that that glowed mysteriously in the dim light. The room was dominated by a massive, circular platform in its center, surrounded by pillars inscribed with complex patterns.

Emily examined the platform closely. "These symbols," she said, "they're different from what we've seen so far. They seem to depict a flow of time rather than just space."

Klaus stepped closer. "It's almost as if this platform is meant to manipulate time. Look at the sequence of these carvings — they suggest a cyclical process, like the turning of a clock."

Apart from the absent Wei as a brilliant linguist, Sophie had already shown her prowess in deciphering the alien language, moved to the control panel beside the platform. "I've seen these symbols before," she said. "They're part of an activation sequence, but there's something more — an additional layer of commands."

The team gathered at the control panel, staring up at the enigmatic carvings. Sophie, her eyes still haunted by the memory of Wei's sacrifice, traced her fingers along the alien stone.

"This is more than a gateway," she murmured, the weight of realization settling in her voice. "It's a time machine."

The others exchanged astonished glances. Time travel — an impossible dream made tangible by the hands of an ancient Martian civilization.

Commander Harris, ever the pragmatic leader, nodded. "Let's be cautious. If this is indeed a time machine, we need to understand how it operates and what safety protocols we should follow."

Ivan agreed. "We don't want to trigger anything that could be harmful. Let's work together to decode this."

Over the next few hours, the team meticulously studied the symbols, combining their expertise to unravel the complex sequence. Sophie played a crucial role in understanding the engineering principles behind the mechanism.

Ivan discovered a key slot, which may be a match for their new acquired Cosmic Key. He said:"Look at this! This may be the lock to our key."

Then Ivan carefully inserted the Cosmic Key, but it had no effect so far.

"It's like a puzzle," Sophie said, her eyes gleaming with excitement. "Each symbol represents a different temporal coordinate. If we align them correctly, we should be able to activate the gate."

The team worked tirelessly, aligning the symbols and inputting the sequence into the control panel. The platform began to hum with energy, and the symbols on the pillars glowed brighter, casting an ethereal light throughout the chamber.

As the final symbol was aligned, the platform began to shift. The floor beneath it parted, revealing a shimmering, translucent gate. The gate was an oval-shaped portal, its surface rippling like water, emanating a soft, blue light.

Emily gasped. "It's beautiful. This must be the time machine gate."

The room filled with a low, resonant hum as the gate stabilized. The room filled with a low, resonant hum as the gate stabilized, as if they were confirming the gate's activation.

Commander Harris stepped forward, his face stern but resolute. "We need to be absolutely sure of what we're dealing with. Let's run some preliminary tests before anyone steps through."

Using the equipment they had brought with them, the team conducted a series of tests on the gate. They analyzed the energy readings, the stability of the portal, and the environmental conditions on the other side.

Klaus and Emily monitored the readings closely. "The energy levels are consistent," Klaus said. "It's stable."

Sophie nodded. "The portal seems to be safe."

The First Step

With the preliminary tests complete, the team faced a critical decision. Who would be the first to step through the gate and explore its potential? The room was silent as they looked at each other, weighing the risks and the excitement of the unknown.

"I'll go," Ivan said, breaking the silence. "As a pilot and a doctor, I can handle whatever we encounter on the other side."

Sophie stepped forward, her eyes locked with Ivan's. "I'll go with you," she said. "We can do this together."

Commander Harris nodded, his respect for their bravery evident. "We'll be right behind you," he said. "Stay in constant communication."

With a deep breath, Ivan and Sophie stepped onto the platform. The team watched as they approached the shimmering gate, their forms gradually becoming translucent as they passed through the portal. The gate rippled and then stabilized, leaving the remaining astronauts to wait anxiously for the first report from the other side.

As Ivan and Sophie disappeared into the portal, the central chamber's hum seemed to grow softer, as if the pyramid itself was holding its breath. The team waited, their hearts pounding, ready to follow their colleagues into the unknown and unlock the final mysteries of the A'kara civilization.

Suddenly there was a flash of lightning and Sophie and Ivan were back with their friends.

Commander Harris asked:"What happened?"

Emily replied frightened:"Obviously we just had some kind of power blackout."

Commander Harris asked:"Are you both alright?"

Sophie spoke in a firm voice:"Yes, Sir! We are fine."

Sophie, being quite the engineer, stepped purposefully towards the console: "Something seems to be wrong with the power supply. Even if A'kara's electricity principles work differently to ours, I'll have to see if I can use something as a relay. I'll have to use something to improvise.

Commander Harris intervened:"No, that's completely out of the question. We'll have to work on a solution thoroughly first. Only then will we give it a try again. That's enough for today. We're breaking off. Let's hit the road and go back to the habitat now."

Chapter 21: The Temporal Passage

The Pyramid's Whispers

The next sol, the five astronauts stood before the gate again inside the Martian pyramid, its complex mechanisms whirring. The discovery of the time travel portal had stunned them all. Ancient hieroglyphs suggested it was a "Temporal Passage," a relic of the A'kara civilization's mastery over time and space.

Commander Harris, Emily, Ivan, Sophie and Klaus exchanged uncertain glances. The possibilities and dangers of such a device weighed heavily on her mind.

Commander Harris remarked:"We've come this far. If the A'kara used this portal, there must be a reason. We need to understand their history and to find it out."

Emily nodded:"Agreed. But we must be cautious. This isn't just an archaeological find; it's a potential key to understanding the universe."

Ivan demanded:"Let's make sure our suits and communication devices are functioning properly. If we get separated, we need a way to stay connected."

With nods of agreement, the team conducted final checks on their equipment. The anticipation was palpable as they gathered in a circle, ready to step into the unknown.

Sophie suggested:"We should set a destination. The hieroglyphs mention a significant event in the A'kara timeline — the Great Transition. It might give us answers."

Klaus said:"I'll configure the portal's interface. Stand by."

Klaus approached the control panel, a series of touch-sensitive glyphs and crystalline knobs. He deciphered the symbols, inputting coordinates for the time period they sought. The portal responded with a hum, and the shimmering energy field solidified into a swirling vortex of light and shadow.

Sophie said anxiously:" There is no way back now. Stay close, everyone."

One by one, the astronauts stepped into the vortex. A sensation of weightlessness enveloped them, followed by a dizzying rush of colors and shapes. It felt as though they were being stretched and compressed simultaneously, a surreal journey through the fabric of space-time.

The vortex spat them out onto solid ground. They stumbled slightly, disoriented but unharmed. As their vision cleared, they found themselves in a vibrant, bustling city — ancient yet advanced, teeming with life.

The Great Transition

Towering spires of crystalline structures rose into the sky, their surfaces shimmering with intricate patterns. The streets below bustled with A'kara citizens, their graceful forms adorned in flowing robes that glowed faintly. The air was filled with a harmonious hum, the energy of the city itself resonating with the frequency of life.

Emily spoke with awe:"Incredible. We're seeing the A'kara civilization at its peak."

Sophie was also impressed and said:"Look at the technology. It's seamlessly integrated with nature. They achieved a balance we can only dream of."

As they marveled at their surroundings, an A'kara figure approached them. Tall and elegant, with a serene expression, the being exuded an aura of wisdom.

The A'kara greeted:"Welcome, travelers from afar. I am Eryon, a keeper of our history. You seek knowledge of the Great Transition."

Commander Harris stepped forward, his voice steady. "Yes, Eryon. We come from a future where your civilization's remnants hold great mysteries. We wish to understand the choices you made."

Eryon nodded, gesturing for them to follow. "Come. I will show you the pivotal moments that shaped our destiny."

Eryon led them through the city, pointing out various landmarks and explaining their significance. The astronauts listened intently, absorbing every detail.

They arrived at a grand plaza, where a colossal structure stood — a fusion of temple and laboratory, pulsating with energy. Eryon paused before it, turning to face the group.

Eryon resumed speaking:"This is the Nexus of Continuity, where the Great Transition began. Our planet was facing entropy, a slow but inevitable decline. Our greatest minds gathered here to seek a solution."

Eryon touched a crystalline panel, and the structure responded by projecting a holographic display. Scenes of A'kara scientists and philosophers debating, working tirelessly, and testing various theories played out before them.

Eryon continued:"We discovered a way to transcend our physical forms, merging our consciousness with the very essence of the planet. This allowed us to preserve our knowledge and existence beyond the limitations of our bodies."

The astronauts watched in awe as the holographic representation of the A'kara's transition unfolded. They saw the initial resistance, the debates on morality and identity, and the eventual consensus that led to the collective merging.

Ivan was impressed:"They faced extinction and chose to become one with their world. It's a profound decision."

Sophie:"And it left behind a civilization encoded in the fabric of Mars. Their knowledge, their essence — it's all here."

Eryon continued, showing the final moments before the transition. The citizens gathered in the plaza, their faces a mixture of hope and sorrow. As the process began, beams of light connected each individual to the Nexus, their forms dissolving into pure energy.

As the holographic display faded, Eryon turned to the astronauts with a serene smile. "This is the legacy we left behind. Our essence exists in harmony with the cosmos, guiding and preserving the balance of existence."

Commander Harris looked at his team, each member deep in thought. "Thank you, Eryon. Your story is a gift to us and to future generations."

Eryon nodded, a look of understanding passing between them. "Your journey is just beginning, travelers. May you find the wisdom to use this knowledge wisely."

The Wisdom of Eryon

As the astronauts prepared to leave the place, Eryon shared one final piece of wisdom with them, emphasizing lessons that transcended time and space:

1. Harmony with Nature: The A'kara achieved their advanced civilization by living in harmony with their environment. Eryon encouraged the astronauts to seek balance and sustainability in their endeavors on Earth and beyond.

Eryon warned:"Technology should not dominate nature but coexist with it, enhancing the beauty and balance of the world."

2. Unity and Collective Wisdom: The success of the A'kara's Great Transition was rooted in their ability to come together, despite differences, to achieve a common goal. Eryon stressed the importance of unity and collective wisdom.

Eryon advised:"True progress is achieved not through individual glory but through collective effort and shared understanding."

3. Adaptability and Resilience: The A'kara faced immense challenges and chose a path that required them to adapt and evolve. Eryon highlighted the need for adaptability and resilience in the face of adversity.

Eryon explained:"Change is the only constant. Embrace it with resilience and an open mind, for it leads to growth and new possibilities."

4. Preservation of Knowledge: The A'kara ensured their legacy by embedding their knowledge within the very fabric of Mars. Eryon advised the astronauts to prioritize the preservation and dissemination of knowledge for future generations.

Eryon reommended:"Knowledge is the true treasure of any civilization. Preserve it, pass it on and teach it to those who come after you."

5. Empathy and Compassion: The A'kara's decision to merge their consciousnesses was rooted in a deep sense of empathy and compassion for one another. Eryon urged the astronauts to cultivate these qualities in their interactions and decision-making.

Eryon stated:"Compassion and empathy are the foundations of a just and prosperous society. Let them guide your actions and choices."

As Eryon's form began to fade, the team felt a profound sense of responsibility. They had not only uncovered the mysteries of an ancient civilization but also received timeless wisdom to guide humanity's future.

Commander Harris gratefully answered:"Thank you, Eryon. We will carry your teachings with us and strive to build a better future for all."

With a final gesture, Eryon activated the portal. The astronauts stepped into the vortex, the vibrant city and its serene inhabitants fading into the swirling light.

When they returned to their time in the pyramid, they were greeted by the familiar surroundings of the ancient structure. The journey through time had left them profoundly changed, their minds brimming with new insights and a deeper understanding of the A'kara civilization.

Commander Harris:"We've seen their greatness and their sacrifice. Now, it's up to us to honor their legacy and continue the exploration of Mars and beyond."

Chapter 22: The Time Portal into the History of Mankind

The Alignment

As the Martian twilight deepened, the stars aligned in a configuration that matched the carvings on the pyramid. Emily tried to decipher the hieroglyphics.

"The hieroglyphs," she said, her voice a mix of excitement and caution, "encode temporal coordinates. We can choose any moment in Earth's history."

Klaus, ever the cautious scientist, frowned. "But what if we alter the past? The consequences —"

Sophie interrupted, her tone resolute. "We'll be observers. The timeline remains intact."

Emily stepped forward and beamed triumphantly:"Well, well, well, Klaus! Have we really found a gap in your education? Have you never learned anything about Albert Einstein's special theory of relativity and the grandfather paradox?" After blinking at Klaus, she said: "Now I'm disappointed in you!"

Emily followed up when she noticed Klaus' uncertain look: "The grandfather paradox is a hypothetical scenario often used to illustrate the potential inconsistencies and contradictions inherent in time travel. The paradox is named after a simple yet profound thought experiment: Imagine a person, let's call them "Time Traveler," who travels back in time and kills their grandfather before the grandfather has any children. This action would prevent the existence of one of the Time Traveler's parents, and consequently, the Time Traveler themselves. But if the Time Traveler never exists, then they could not have traveled back in time to commit the act in the first place. This creates a logical inconsistency, as it leads to a situation where the Time Traveler both exists and does not exist simultaneously."

Klaus smiled back to Emily:"Alright, I give up! You are too smart for me, Emily."

Ivan stepped forward, his gaze fixed on the shimmering time machine gate. "We lost Wei recently," he said, his voice filled with determination. "We won't lose anybody else again."

Sophie nodded. "We owe it to her. We need to understand the full scope of this technology."

The Jump Back in Time

The team formed a circle, holding hands as they prepared for the next leap into the unknown. Sophie whispered the activation phrase — the alien words opened the gate. Insights into the earth's past were revealed: ancient civilizations, wars, revolutions.

"Choose an event that shaped us," Sophie called out to Emily.

Emily closed her eyes, focusing on a pivotal moment in human history — the birth of modern science. "Galileo," she said, her voice filled with awe. "Florence, 1610."

Their objective was clear: to witness the moment when Galileo Galilei first pointed his telescope at the night sky, a moment that would forever change humanity's understanding of the universe.

The pyramid pulsed with energy, and they stepped through the portal.

They materialized in the midst of a bustling city. The architecture and clothes of the people around them suggested they had arrived in Florence.

The narrow, cobblestone streets of Florence were alive with activity. Merchants peddled their goods, artists painted in open-air studios, and scholars debated in the piazzas. The air was filled with the scent of fresh bread and the sound of church bells ringing in the distance.

"This is incredible," Emily whispered, her eyes wide with wonder. "We have really traveled back in history."

Sophie, her mind already working to absorb as much information as possible, added, "We need to be careful. Our presence here must remain unnoticed."

When dusk fell, they made their way through the city, following the path that would lead them to Galileo's villa.

They entered a moonlit garden, the air filled with the scents of night-blooming flowers and the distant murmur of the Arno River.

In the garden stood Galileo, hunched over his telescope, peering intently at the stars. Sophie gasped in awe.

"The father of modern astronomy," she whispered, her voice tinged with reverence.

Ivan grinned, the tension of the journey easing slightly. "And Sophie's distant relative, if I'm not mistaken."

The Forbidden Conversation

They watched as Galileo traced the moons of Jupiter, his face alight with discovery. The four largest moons (Io, Europa, Ganymede and Callisto) were later named the Galilean moons in his honor. Unable to contain her excitement, Emily approached him cautiously and was the first to speak.

"Galileo Galilei?" she called softly, not wanting to startle him.

The old man turned, his brows furrowing in curiosity. "Who is there?" he asked in Italian, his voice strong despite his age.

Galileo squinted at her, his eyes sharp with curiosity and suspicion. "Witches?" he asked, his voice wary.

"No," Klaus interjected quickly. "Explorers. Scientists like you."

Emily stepped forward, a warm smile on her face. "My name is Emily. We come from a place far away, and we have traveled a great distance to meet you."

Galileo's eyes narrowed slightly, studying the group of strangely dressed individuals before him. "You are not from these lands," he observed. "Your attire is... peculiar. Who are you truly?"

Commander Harris stepped forward, his expression respectful but firm. "We are explorers, scientists like yourself. We have come to learn from you and perhaps share some of our own knowledge."

Galileo's curiosity was piqued. He motioned for them to come closer, away from the telescope. "Very well," he said, "but you must explain more, for your presence here is most unusual."

As they gathered around a small wooden table adorned with star charts and notes, Galileo spoke passionately about his recent discoveries. "I have been observing the heavens through my telescope," he began, his eyes shining with fervor. "Just tonight, I have made an extraordinary observation—the moons of Jupiter."

Sophie leaned in, her eyes wide with amazement. "The moons of Jupiter? You have seen them move?"

Galileo nodded, a triumphant smile spreading across his face. "Indeed. I have tracked their movement and noted their positions. They orbit Jupiter, much like our own moon orbits Earth. This, I believe, is proof that not all celestial bodies revolve around the Earth."

Emily couldn't contain her excitement. "Your discovery is groundbreaking, Galileo. It will change the way humanity understands the cosmos."

Galileo looked intrigued. "You speak as if you know what the future holds. How is this possible?"

Ivan, always cautious, stepped in. "We have knowledge from a time beyond your own. Your work lays the foundation for future astronomers and scientists. You are a pioneer."

Galileo's eyes widened with a mix of disbelief and wonder. "You mean to say... I am remembered? My work endures?"

Commander Harris nodded. "Indeed, your name is known and respected for centuries. Your courage to challenge established beliefs inspires countless others."

Klaus, the scientist of the group, leaned forward. "Galileo, your observations support the heliocentric model proposed by Copernicus, do they not?"

Galileo's expression grew serious. "Yes, but it is a dangerous belief to hold. The Church strongly opposes such ideas. They insist that Earth is the center of the universe."

Sophie spoke softly but firmly. "Sometimes, the truth must be defended, even at great personal risk. Your work is too important to be suppressed."

Galileo sighed, a mixture of determination and resignation in his eyes. "I know this, and yet, the consequences of defying the Church are severe. I must tread carefully."

Emily reached out, placing a hand on Galileo's arm. "We understand the danger you face. Know that you are not alone. Your discoveries will eventually find their rightful place in history."

Galileo nodded, a sense of solidarity forming between him and the astronauts. "Thank you, my friends. Your words give me strength. I will continue my work, no matter the cost."

Sophie leaned in closer. "Galileo, your courage in the face of adversity is inspiring. How do you find the strength to continue your work, knowing the risks?"

Galileo smiled softly, a glint of determination in his eyes. "The pursuit of truth is a noble endeavor. I have always believed that understanding the universe is a way to honor the Creator. How can we not seek to know the beauty of His work?"

Klaus, nodding, added, "In our time, many scientists face similar challenges. The pursuit of knowledge often conflicts with established beliefs. But your example shows that progress is worth the struggle."

Galileo's expression softened with gratitude. "It is heartening to know that future generations continue this quest. Tell me, what wonders have you discovered?"

Ivan shared cautiously, "We have explored beyond our own planet, sending machines and people to other worlds. We have seen moons, planets, and even stars up close. Your work laid the groundwork for these achievements."

Galileo listened, his eyes wide with wonder and disbelief. "Tell me," he said, "what lies beyond the stars?"

Emily hesitated, aware of the delicate balance they must maintain. "A universe of wonders," she replied carefully. "But some secrets are best left undiscovered, for now."

Galileo's eyes widened in awe. "To travel among the stars... it is a dream I have often pondered. Your words fill me with hope for what is to come."

Emily, feeling a deep connection, said, "Your legacy is vast, Galileo. Your discoveries about Jupiter's moons will lead to a greater understanding of our place in the cosmos. You have shown us that the pursuit of knowledge is a journey worth taking."

Galileo's gaze grew intense. "Promise me that you will continue this journey, no matter the obstacles. The truth must prevail, for the benefit of all humanity."

Commander Harris, with a solemn nod, replied, "We promise, Galileo. Your work will inspire us to push the boundaries of our knowledge and to seek the truth, no matter the cost."

As the night grew deeper, the astronauts knew it was time to leave. They had shared their knowledge and offered encouragement, but they could not stay. Galileo escorted them back to the spot where they had first appeared.

"Take care, Galileo," Sophie said, her voice filled with admiration. "The world needs your brilliance."

"And remember," Emily added, "the stars you study will one day be studied by those based on your findings."

As the team prepared to return to the pyramid, Emily lingered, her heart heavy with unspoken words. She stepped closer to Galileo, her voice soft and earnest.

"Galileo," she whispered, "keep looking up. Your work will change the world."

He nodded, a flicker of understanding and inspiration in his eyes, though he couldn't fully grasp the enormity of her words.

With a final nod, Galileo watched as the astronauts activated their device, a soft hum filling the air as they disappeared from his time. As he returned to his telescope, Galileo's heart was filled with renewed determination and hope. He knew now that his work would transcend time, lighting the way for future generations.

Back on Mars, the team reappeared in the familiar confines of the pyramid. They held hands once more, the experience binding them together in a new and profound way.

Emily meticulously documented their encounter with Galileo, her writing infused with the wonder and inspiration of the Renaissance scientist. Klaus and Emily found solace in the shared memories, their bond strengthened by the trials they had faced together.

The pyramid whispered in their minds:"Time is a river. We are its ripples."

The astronauts had become chrononauts, weaving through the fabric of time. Their journey had just begun, each step a ripple in the vast river of existence, carrying the wisdom and legacy of both Earth and Mars. This trip back in time to Galileo left such a strong impression that the astronauts were already planning another visit to this important figure in history. To do so, they chose a significant event that has also become an indelible part of the history books.

Chapter 23: Galileo's Trial (1633)

Arrival in Rome

The Martian pyramid's time machine gate shimmered and pulsed as the team prepared for their next journey through time. They had selected another crucial moment in the history of science: Galileo Galilei's trial before the Inquisition in 1633. As the stars aligned once more, the portal opened, revealing the harsh light and echoing halls of the Roman Inquisition's chambers.

The team materialized in a shadowed corner of the chamber, unseen by the gathered officials and onlookers. The room was a stark contrast to the Martian pyramid, filled with the weight of history and the oppressive atmosphere of fear and authority. At the center stood Galileo, his face lined with age and worry, his once-bright eyes dimmed by the prospect of condemnation.

Sophie stepped forward, her resolve steeling her nerves. "We can't interfere directly," she whispered to the team, "but we can offer Galileo the moral support and arguments he needs."

Emily nodded, her passion for science burning brighter than ever. "We need to make them see reason, to understand the truth of heliocentrism."

Klaus, ever the pragmatist, remained silent but observant, his mind torn between the desire to preserve history and the pursuit of truth.

The Inquisition Begins

The trial commenced with the inquisitors reading the charges against Galileo: heresy and disobedience for advocating the heliocentric model of the universe. The room was filled with the low murmur of disapproval and fear from the gathered crowd.

Galileo stood alone, a solitary figure against the might of the Church. But as Sophie, Emily, and Klaus watched, they knew they had to find a way to support him.

Sophie's Support

Sophie moved closer, her presence unseen but her voice carrying the weight of conviction. "Galileo," she whispered, "you must stand firm. We are with you."

Galileo, though unaware of the source of the voice, seemed to draw strength from it. He raised his head, his voice steady. "I have only sought the truth," he declared. "The observations I have made with my telescope confirm the heliocentric model proposed by Coperni cus."

The inquisitors shifted uneasily. One of them, an older man with a stern face, seemed to waver.

Klaus watched the proceedings. He understood the danger of inter- fering with the past but also saw the potential to influence minds towards truth and reason. He noted the inquisitors' body language, searching for any sign of doubt or openness to persuasion.

As the arguments continued, Klaus saw an opportunity. He moved closer to the inquisitor who had shown signs of wavering. "You know this is the truth," he whispered in his ear, using his knowledge of human psychology. "Science cannot be silenced."

The Turning Point

The Inquisitor looked around, his face troubled, he saw nobody, had his conscience whispered to him?
"Galileo," he said, his voice softer, "you have made remarkable observations, but the Church cannot condone teachings that contradict Scripture."

Galileo's face fell, but Sophie, sensing the moment of weakness, spoke again. "Ask them to look through the telescope," she urged.

Galileo nodded, desperation and hope mingling in his eyes. "I ask only that you look through the telescope yourselves," he said. "See what I have seen."

Reluctantly, the inquisitors agreed. A telescope was brought into the chamber, and one by one, they looked through it, their expressions shifting from skepticism to wonder. The moons of Jupiter, the phases of Venus — they could not deny the evidence before their eyes.

The Verdict

After a tense silence, the lead inquisitor spoke. "Galileo, your findings are remarkable. However, the Roman Catholic Church must maintain its authority. You will be allowed to continue your work, but you must do so in private, without publicizing your findings."

Galileo nodded, relief and disappointment mingling on his face. It was not a full victory, but it was a step towards the eventual acceptance of heliocentrism.

As a matter of fact, in 1822 first, the Congregation of the Holy Office (the Inquisition) formally allowed the publication of books that treated heliocentrism as a physical fact rather than just a hypothesis. This was followed by an official decree from Pope Pius VII in 1820, which was subsequently published in 1822. It was not until 1992 that Pope John Paul II formally acknowledged the Church's error in condemning Galileo. This act was part of a broader initiative to reconcile the Catholic Church with modern science.

Return to Mars

As the trial concluded, the team felt the pull of the pyramid's gateway. They had done what they could without altering the course of history too drastically. They stepped back into the portal, the room dissolving into the familiar hum of the Martian pyramid.

Back on Mars, the team stood in silence, processing the experience of their journey. Emily felt a deep sense of fulfillment, knowing they had supported one of the greatest minds in history. Sophie and Klaus shared a look of mutual respect and understanding.

"We did what we could," Ivan said softly. "We helped him stand firm in his convictions."

"And in time," Sophie added, "the truth will prevail."

The pyramid whispered to them once more: "Time is a river. We are its ripples."

And with that, they knew their journey was far from over.

Chapter 24: Encounter with Legendary Robin Hood (12th Century)

The astronauts were impressed by the possibility of time travel and planned to do more to broaden their horizons. Emily, their designated historian and tour guide, wanted to pay a visit to her home country. She had been fascinated by Robin Hood's adventures in her school days.

Robin Hood is best known for:
1) He is the legendary outlaw hero who "steals from the rich and gives to the poor".
2) The rescue of Maid Marian, his romantic love, a noblewoman who becomes embroiled in the conflict between Robin Hood and his adversaries, particularly the Sheriff of Nottingham.
3) An arrow is shot to split another arrow that is already stuck in a target. This extraordinary display of archery skill is known as "splitting the arrow" or the "Robin Hood shot".

The team agreed to follow Emily to medieval England. With a sense of anticipation, the astronauts prepared for their encounter with the legendary outlaw. Each carried a discreet recording device, concealed within their garments, to document their encounter without altering the course of history.

Sophie input the temporal coordinates into the gateway's control panel, activating the ancient technology with a soft hum. The gateway shimmered, revealing glimpses of medieval England. With a shared sense of purpose, they stepped into the time vortex, ready to embark on their quest to Nottingham.

"Let us approach this meeting with caution and respect," Commander Harris urged, his voice carrying the weight of their mission.

Nottingham and the Rescue of Maid Marian

The astronauts materialized in a dimly lit alley in the bustling town of Nottingham. The cobblestone streets were alive with the sounds of merchants hawking their wares, townsfolk chatting, and the clinking armor of the Sheriff's guards. The scent of freshly baked bread mingled with the earthy aroma of the nearby forest.

Sophie exclaimed excitedly:"This is incredible! We're really here, in medieval England."

Commander Harris warned his group:"Stay alert, everyone. We don't know what or who we might encounter here."

Commander Harris scanned the area. He continued to say:"We need to find Maid Marian. According to the legends, she's being held in the Sheriff's castle."

"Let's gather information discreetly," Emily suggested. "We don't want to draw attention to ourselves."

As they moved through the crowded marketplace, they overheard whispers of Maid Marian's imminent execution. The Sheriff of Nottingham had accused her of aiding Robin Hood and planned to make an example of her.

The Plan

"We don't have much time," Sophie said urgently. "We need a plan to get inside the castle and free her."

"I can use the cloaking bracelet to scout the area and find her exact location," Klaus offered.

"Sophie and I will take the plasma scepter," Ivan said. "We'll handle the guards."

"I'll stay with Sophie and Emily," Commander Harris said. "We'll use the medical rod to ensure Marian's safe escape."

Klaus slipped on the cloaking bracelet, instantly becoming a barely perceptible shimmer. He moved swiftly towards the castle, slipping past the guards undetected.

Infiltrating the Castle

Inside the castle, Klaus navigated through dark corridors, avoiding the patrolling guards. He found Maid Marian in a small, dimly lit cell. She was chained to the wall, her face pale but resolute.

Klaus deactivated the cloaking device and appeared before her. "We're here to help," he whispered.

Maid Marian's eyes widened in surprise. "Who are you?"

Maid Marian bore a certain resemblance to Emily, so Klaus thought the two women could be relatives, even though time definitely doesn't make this possible. But who knows? The biologist Klaus was tempted to do a DNA analysis of Maid Marian in order to prove Emily's genetic descent from Maid Marian.

"A friend," Klaus replied, using the bracelet to become invisible again. "I'll be back with help."

The Rescue Mission

Outside the castle, the team waited in the shadows. Klaus reappeared and briefed them on Maid Marian's location.

"Sophie, Ivan, take out the guards at the entrance," Commander Harris instructed. "Emily and Sophie, follow me."

Sophie adjusted the plasma scepter to stun mode. With precise shots, she and Ivan incapacitated the guards at the entrance, clearing a path for the others. They moved quickly through the castle, using the cloaking bracelet to avoid detection.

They reached the dungeon without incident. Sophie and Emily used the bracelet to slip past the guards and unlock Maid Marian's cell. Commander Harris used the medical rod to heal Maid Marian's wounds, and she regained her strength instantly.

"We need to move fast," Maid Marian said. "The Sheriff's men will be here any minute."

The Fight

As they made their way back to the castle entrance, the alarm was raised. Guards flooded the corridors, weapons drawn. Commander Harris switched the plasma scepter to burn mode, using controlled bursts to clear a path. Ivan and Klaus engaged in close combat, while Sophie and Emily used the cloaking bracelet to create confusion, appearing and disappearing, striking from the shadows.

Despite the odds, their advanced technology and teamwork prevailed. The guards were quickly overwhelmed, allowing the group to escape the castle and melt into the town.

Meeting Friar Tuck

In the chaos, they encountered a rotund, bald-head man in monk's

robes — Friar Tuck. He had a friendly, jovial expression, and a
wooden cross hung around his neck.

Friar Tuck noticed the astronauts and addressed them:"Well, well,
what do we have here? Travelers from afar, it seems."

Emily stepped forward and answered:"Greetings. We are indeed travelers, though our journey is quite unconventional. My name is Emily, and these are my companions, Commander Harris, Ivan, Sophie, and Klaus."

Friar Tuck with a twinkle in his eye commented:"Unconventional, you say? You look like no travelers I have ever seen. Your attire is most curious. Are your knights of sorts as you wear these peculiar armors and helmets?"

Klaus:"In our world the knights are called "astronauts", and our armors and helmets are called "space suits". We come from a place far from here, both in distance and time. We mean no harm and seek only knowledge and understanding. And right now, we need a safe shelter for this lady." Klaus brought Maid Marian forward, whom he had previously kept hidden behind his stocky stature.

Recognizing Maid Marian and seeing the strangers helping her, Friar Tuck quickly joined their group.

Friar Tuck nodded and said:"Ah, seekers of knowledge. A noble pursuit. You must be weary from your travels. Come, let us find you some rest and nourishment. I shall take you to my friends. They will be most interested to meet you."

"Follow me," he urged, leading them through the maze-like streets to a hidden path that led into Sherwood Forest.

Under the canopy of ancient trees, the atmosphere shifted from tense urgency to cautious relief. Friar Tuck, now more relaxed, turned to Maid Marian. "Robin will be glad to see you safe, my lady. And who might your friends be?"

Meeting the Legend: Robin Hood and his Merry Men in Sherwood Forest

"Welcome to Sherwood Forest," Emily whispered, her eyes scanning the verdant landscape. "This is the domain of Robin Hood and his band of merry men."

The air was cool and filled with the scent of pine and damp earth. Birds chirped in the distance, and the sound of rustling leaves hinted at the presence of wildlife. The astronauts, still in their suits but with visors open, looked around in awe at the lush greenery surrounding them.

The astronauts followed Friar Tuck through the forest, marveling at the beauty of their surroundings. The trees were tall and ancient, their leaves forming a dense canopy overhead. After a short walk, they arrived at a hidden camp, bustling with activity. Men and women in rustic clothing moved about, some tending to chores while others practiced archery or sparred with wooden swords.

Friar Tuck approached a hooded man with a quiver full of arrows and a bow. Was this the legendary, much sought-after figure of legend, the reason for their journey through time? His height was impressive by the standards of the time.

Robin Hood posed the question to Friar Tuck:"Tuck, who are these strangers you bring to our camp?"

Friar Tuck grinned and replied:"Robin, these are travelers from a faraway land. In their world, the knights are called "astronauts", and their apparel of armors and helmets are called "space suits". Their story is most intriguing, and I thought you would like to hear it. Furthermore, they rescued Maid Marian from the evil clutches of the Sheriff of Nottingham and brought her back here unharmed."

A tall figure with a confident bearing stepped forward, a bow slung over his shoulder. His piercing eyes scrutinized the newcomers. "Marian," he said with a smile. "Welcome back. And who are these brave souls?"

"Robin, these are our new allies," Maid Marian said. "They call themselves astronauts, whatever that means. But they have skills and tools I've never seen before. They helped me escape."

Robin Hood studied the astronauts and said, "Welcome to Sherwood Forest. I am Robin Hood, and these are my Merry Men. We stand against tyranny and fight for justice. Anyone who helps my lady is a friend of mine." Robin Hood held out his hand to Commander Harris.

Commander Harris shook his hand firmly and began:"We're honored to meet you, Robin. We come from a distant land, but for now, we share a common cause."

"Robin Hood," Commander Harris restarted, his voice filled with respect, "we've traveled through time to seek your wisdom and guidance. Your courage and generosity have inspired generations, and once again, we are honored to meet you."

Robin Hood regarded them with a mixture of curiosity and skepticism, his keen eyes assessing each member of the group.

"What business do travelers from distant lands have with me?" he asked, his voice tinged with suspicion. "Ah, travelers in search of wisdom, are you? And what do you hope to learn from an outlaw such as myself?"

Emily stepped forward, her gaze steady and determined. "We seek to understand the principles of justice and equality that you stand for," she explained. "Your actions have challenged the oppressive forces of tyranny and injustice, and we hope to learn from your example."

Emily, with her impeccable British English accent, could have perfectly mingled in with people living here, although centuries separated them.

Robin Hood said:"You look so similar to Marian. Are you twin sisters?" Klaus smiled, as he obtained a confirmation of his previous impression, when he first met Maid Marian.

Emily replied with a twinkle in her eyes:"You flatter me, Robin! But we are not."

Robin Hood continued:"Alright, then. Justice and equality, you say? They are noble ideals indeed, but they are not easily attained. The road to justice is fraught with danger and uncertainty. Are you prepared to walk that path?"

Ivan:"We are, Robin Hood. We believe that justice is worth fighting for, even in the face of adversity."

Robin Hood:"Spoken like true warriors, my friends. But remember, the path of justice is not always clear-cut. Sometimes, we must make difficult choices and sacrifices for the greater good."

Sophie now also joined in:"We understand, Robin Hood. We are prepared to face whatever challenges lie ahead in our quest for justice."

Robin Hood looked at her for a moment and then nodded in acknowledgment. "Very well," he said, his tone softening. "My friends, sit with us, and I will tell you tales of bravery and heroism."

Robin Hood introduced his Merry Men to the travelers:"Welcome, friends. You have traveled far to reach us, and it is our honor to share this night with you. Allow me to introduce my companions: Little John, my loyal right hand; you know already Friar Tuck, our spiritual guide; Will Scarlett, the fleet-footed; and Alan-a-Dale, the minstrel with a voice as sweet as honey."

The astronauts felt a deep connection to this legendary hero and his band of outlaws — the Merry Men. They had bridged time and space to stand beside legendary Robin Hood, united in the struggle for justice and freedom.

Commander Harris:" We have heard of your legendary deeds and wish to learn from your experiences."

Little John stepped forward:"And what tales do you have to share, travelers? You must have seen much in your journeys."

Ivan interjected:"Indeed, we have. We come from a distant future where the world is vastly different. We have faced many challenges and learned many lessons, but there is always more to discover."

Will Scarlett smiled:"Then you have come to the right place. There is much we can teach each other. Come, sit by the fire and share your tales."

The travelers gathered around the campfire, their faces illuminated by the flickering flames. Robin Hood settled himself on a fallen log.

Robin Hood began to speak:"Listen closely, my friends, for I will tell you of the injustices that have plagued our land for far too long, and of the brave souls who have dared to stand against them..."

And so, beneath the canopy of Sherwood Forest, Robin Hood regaled the travelers with tales of daring escapades, valiant deeds, and acts of selfless heroism. As the night wore on, they listened intently, their hearts filled with admiration for the legendary outlaw and his band of Merry Men.

The Meaning of Archery

Robin Hood explained:"Archery, my friends, is not merely the act of loosing an arrow from a bow. It is a symbol — a symbol of skill, precision, and discipline. It is a craft that demands both strength of body and clarity of mind."

Emily asked:"But what does archery signify beyond its physical aspects, Robin Hood? What deeper meaning does it hold?"

Robin Hood replied:"Ah, an astute question, my dear. Archery, you see, is more than just a means of hunting or warfare. It is a metaphor for life itself."

Ivan interjected:"How so, Robin Hood? I fail to see the connection between archery and the complexities of life."

Robin Hood tried to clarify:"Consider this, Ivan. When one draws back the bowstring, they must focus their mind and steady their hand. They must align their aim with their intention, and release the arrow with purpose and conviction. In that moment, there is no room for doubt or hesitation. There is only the arrow, flying true towards its target."

Sophie concluded:"So, archery is a metaphor for staying focused and determined in the face of adversity?"

Robin Hood nodded:"Precisely, Sophie. In life, as in archery, we are often faced with obstacles and challenges that threaten to throw us off course. But if we remain steadfast in our purpose, if we keep our eyes fixed on the target, then we can overcome even the greatest of trials."

Klaus asked with a skeptical look on his face:"What of the arrow itself? What does it symbolize?"

Robin Hood replied:"The arrow, my friend, is a symbol of hope — a beacon of light in the darkness. It represents our dreams, our aspirations, and our relentless pursuit of a better tomorrow. With every shot we take, we inch closer to our goals, our hopes soaring ever higher like arrows in flight."

Klaus said to his fellow astronauts:"It's a shame Wei can't take part in this discussion, because she could have contributed her knowledge of archery with a background in Zen Buddhism."

Emily's look could have killed Klaus. How could he mention Wei again. She wondered: Is Wei still in his thoughts with love and affection? It was still not enough. Emily was aware that she would have to get Klaus to make a clear commitment to her when the opportunity arose.

The astronauts and the Merry Men share a moment of camaraderie, their spirits lifted by the exchange of ideas and the shared commitment to justice. The campfire burns low, and the stars above Sherwood Forest twinkle brightly, witnesses to this extraordinary meeting.

Emily brought up the archery topic again:"Robin Hood was explaining to us the deeper meaning of archery. We are curious to learn more about your philosophies and how they can guide us in our own journey." As Emily posed this question, she both thought and wished that Klaus would recognize that she could ask equally clever questions about the philosophy of archery. Wei wouldn't be needed for that.

Will Scarlett took over the conversation:"Archery is indeed a noble art, but it is just one aspect of our way of life. There is much more to be learned here in Sherwood."

Alan-a-Dale interjected:"Let me share a song that speaks of our struggles and triumphs. Music has a way of conveying truths that words alone cannot."

Alan-a-Dale strums his lute and begins to sing a ballad about the Merry Men's exploits, their battles against the Sheriff of Nottingham, and their unwavering commitment to the people.

Motivation to Take Action

Ivan, who is a musician himself, said:"That was beautiful, Alan. Your music truly captures the spirit of your cause. But I am curious — what drives each of you to fight for justice? What motivates you to take such great risks, Robin Hood?"

Robin Hood's eyes softened with nostalgia. He took a deep breath, his mind traveling back to distant lands and old battles.

"My story begins long before I became an outlaw," he started, his voice steady and reflective. "I was born Robert of Locksley, a nobleman with a comfortable life. But my world changed when I joined King Richard the Lionheart on the Third Crusade. I was young and eager, full of ideals about glory and honor."

He paused, the firelight casting shadows across his weathered face. "The Crusades were a brutal affair. I saw things that would haunt any man — cities besieged, lives lost, and a constant struggle against an enemy that was as human as we were. It was in those harsh deserts and bloody battlefields that I earned my skills in archery and combat. But more importantly, it was there that I learned the true cost of war."

Emily leaned forward, her eyes wide with fascination. "And what about King Richard?"

Robin Hood smiled fondly. "Richard was a warrior king, through and through. He was fierce in battle, a true lion at heart. But he was also just and fair, a ruler who inspired loyalty and courage. We shared many battles together, side by side. There was mutual respect between us, a bond forged in the fires of war."

Klaus, always curious about the personal connections, asked, "How did that relationship shape who you are now?"

Robin Hood's expression turned somber. "When we returned to England, we found our homeland in turmoil. Richard was captured on his way back, and while he was imprisoned, his brother John seized power, ruling with tyranny and greed. The England I returned to was not the one I had left. People were suffering, taxed beyond their means, and justice was a rarity."

He clenched his fist, the fire reflecting in his intense gaze. "It was then that I realized my true calling. I could no longer stand by as my people suffered. I took to the forests, gathering like-minded men and women. We became outlaws, yes, but outlaws with a cause — to protect the weak, to fight injustice, and to remind those in power that they are not beyond the reach of accountability."

Sophie nodded, deeply moved by his story. "So, your time with Richard, your experiences as a Crusader, they shaped your sense of justice?"

Robin Hood nodded. "Indeed. The Crusades taught me the value of every life, the importance of fighting for what is right, and the strength of unity. My relationship with Richard taught me the qualities of true leadership and the impact a just ruler can have. When I fight now, I do so with the hope that one day, justice will prevail, and England will know peace again."

Ivan, inspired by Robin Hood's tale, asked, "What advice would you give to us, as travelers from another time, seeking to make a difference?"

Robin Hood looked at each of them, his eyes filled with wisdom and determination. "Stand for what is right, even when it is difficult. Use your skills and knowledge to protect those who cannot protect themselves. And remember, true leadership is not about power, but about serving others. Fight with honor, and never lose sight of your principles. For me, it is the love of the people. Seeing their suffering and knowing I have the power to make a difference compels me to act. The tyranny of the rich and powerful must be challenged, and I will do whatever it takes to protect the innocent."

Little John added:"I fight for loyalty and brotherhood. Robin and I have been through many battles together, and our bond is unbreakable. Our cause is just, and our unity gives us strength."

Friar Tuck commented:"For me, it is a matter of faith. I believe in a higher power that calls us to fight against injustice. The teachings of our faith compel us to act with compassion and to defend the oppressed."

Will Scarlett explained:"Speed and agility are my strengths, and I use them to outsmart our enemies. But my motivation comes from a deep sense of fairness. I cannot stand by and watch as the poor are exploited and mistreated."

Alan-a-Dale contributes to the discussion:"My music is my weapon. Through song, I inspire hope and courage in our comrades. I fight for the joy of seeing our people rise above their struggles and reclaim their dignity."

Klaus said, addressing Robin Hood:"Your words and deeds are truly inspiring. We come from a world where justice is often overshadowed by greed and corruption. What advice would you give us to help us navigate these challenges?"

Robin Hood advised:"Stay true to your principles, no matter the cost. The path of righteousness is not an easy one, but it is the only path worth walking. Be brave, be steadfast, and never lose sight of your goals."

Friar Tuck added:"And remember to seek strength in unity. Alone, we are vulnerable, but together, we are formidable. Surround yourselves with allies who share your vision and values."

Emily:"Thank you, Robin, and thank you all. Your wisdom will guide us as we continue our journey. We are honored to have met you and to have shared in your knowledge."

Robin Hood:"The honor is ours, Emily. And you really are not Marian's sister?"

This was considered a rhetorical question, so Robin Hood did not wait for an answer from anyone and continued:

"May your arrows fly true, and may you find the justice you seek. Remember, Sherwood Forest will always be a haven for those who fight for what is right."

Commander Harris said:"Thank you, Robin Hood, for your wisdom. Your words have given us much to ponder as we continue on our journey."

Robin Hood:"It has been my pleasure, Commander. Remember, my friends, that the true essence of archery lies not in the bullseye, but in the journey — the journey of self-discovery, of growth, and of transformation. So let your arrows fly true, and may your hearts be forever guided by the wisdom of the bow."

As the fire dwindled to embers and the stars began to twinkle overhead, the astronauts bid farewell to Robin Hood and his band of Merry Men. They returned to the present, their hearts filled with gratitude for the opportunity to meet a legend of the past. Their minds were ablaze with the echoes of their timeless wisdom.

"We've witnessed the power of courage and compassion," Emily reflected, her voice filled with reverence. "And in doing so, we've gained a deeper understanding of the enduring spirit of human resilience."

Chapter 25: Exploring Ancient Greece (399 BC)

A Glimpse into Antiquity

Within the depths of the Martian pyramid, the astronauts convened once more, guided by their insatiable thirst for knowledge and adventure. Emily, the team's historian, Emily, the team's historian, suggested the next time travel destination: ancient Greece, during the height of its intellectual and cultural zenith.

"Greece, about 400 BC," Emily announced, her voice brimming with excitement. "We'll bear witness to the birth of democracy, the flourishing of philosophy, and the marvels of ancient architecture."

Eyes alight with anticipation, the team exchanged knowing glances, eager to embark on this extraordinary voyage into the annals of history.

The Martian pyramid's portal once again hummed with ethereal energy as the astronauts prepared for another journey through time. They wanted to meet the famous philosopher Socrates.

The astronauts dressed like the citizens of ancient Greece and blended seamlessly into the past. Each carried a discreet recording device, concealed within their garments, to capture the wonders of this bygone era without disturbing its delicate balance.

Sophie deftly input the temporal coordinates into the gateway's control panel, activating the ancient technology with a gentle hum. The gateway formed a swirling vortex of light before them. Commander

Harris, Emily, Klaus, Sophie and Ivan held their hands in a circle. Sophie whispered the activation phrase and the gateway shimmered, revealing breathtaking glimpses of ancient Athens.

"Let us approach with reverence and humility," Commander Harris urged.

With a shared sense of purpose, they stepped into the vortex, ready to immerse themselves in the wonders of ancient Greece.

Arrival in the Cradle of Civilization

As the vortex dissipated, the astronauts materialized in the heart of ancient Athens.

"Welcome to the birthplace of Western civilization," Emily exclaimed, her eyes sparkling with wonder. "Behold the Acropolis, the Parthenon, and the bustling Agora below."

They marveled at the architectural marvels that surrounded them, their beauty and elegance standing as a testament to the ingenuity and artistic prowess of the ancient Greeks.

Guided by Emily's expertise, the astronauts ventured into the heart of Athenian society, where philosophers debated the nature of existence, poets sang of heroes and gods, and artisans crafted timeless works of art.

"This is a land steeped in wisdom and beauty," Emily remarked, his voice tinged with reverence. "To witness the birth of democracy and the flourishing of intellect is truly awe-inspiring."

As they observed the vibrant tapestry of ancient Greek life, the astronauts felt a profound sense of connection to the past, their presence a silent tribute to the enduring legacy of human creativity and innovation.

"We've walked in the footsteps of giants," Emily mused, her gaze lingering on the ancient buildings.

The Market Chase

They arrived in the bustling Agora, the central marketplace of Athens, surrounded by ancient architecture, merchants, and philosophers engaging in lively debates.

"We need to find Socrates," Commander Harris said, looking around the crowded marketplace. "But we must be careful not to attract attention."

The sun shone brightly over the Agora of Athens, casting a warm glow on the marble columns and vibrant market stalls. Merchants hawked their wares, children ran through the crowd, and the air was filled with the sounds of haggling and laughter.

The Agora was a kaleidoscope of colors and motion. Merchants' stalls lined the streets, overflowing with an array of goods — ceramics painted with intricate designs, bronze and iron tools, fresh produce, and exotic spices from distant lands. Artisans displayed their crafts, from potters shaping clay on their wheels to blacksmiths hammering glowing metal.

Bustling crowds filled every corner, their chatter creating a constant hum of activity. The din of haggling voices, punctuated by the occasional shout of a merchant advertising their wares, blended with the sounds of livestock — sheep bleating, chickens clucking, and the occasional bray of a donkey.

The air was thick with a medley of aromas. The sharp scent of freshly cut herbs mingled with the earthy smell of pottery clay and the tang of animal hides. From the food stalls came the enticing smells of roasted meats, freshly baked bread, and the sweet aroma of honey cakes. The fragrance of olive oil, poured over everything from salads to hot bread, permeated the air, adding to the olfactory tapestry.

The astronauts' presence in the Agora was immediately noticed. Curious eyes turned toward the newcomers. The astronauts, trying to blend in, moved cautiously through the market. Emily, with her bright red hair, and Klaus, with his bald head, drew particular interest. The murmurs of the crowd grew louder, a wave of suspicion rippling through the marketplace, and soon a small crowd had formed around them.

"Who are these people?" a merchant muttered to his neighbor. The questions flew, the crowd's curiosity rapidly turning to unease.

"Look at their clothes! They must be from a distant land," another replied.

Sensing the mounting tension, Commander Harris signaled to his team to move. "We need to get out of here, now."

Sophie, always quick on her feet, activated her cloaking bracelet. She vanished from sight, causing gasps of astonishment from the onlookers. Using her invisibility to create a distraction, she knocked over a fruit cart. Apples and oranges scattered across the ground, causing a commotion and drawing the attention of the guards.

"Go! Now!" Sophie's disembodied voice urged the team.

Taking advantage of the chaos, the astronauts slipped away, blending into the throng of market-goers.

The city guards, alerted by the commotion, began to close in. Their armor clanked as they pushed through the crowd, determined to apprehend the strangers. The astronauts, now a target, had no choice but to flee.

Commander Harris led the way, using the plasma scepter in stun mode to disable any guards that got too close. The bright flashes of the scepter's energy pulses cut through the dimming light, each shot sending a guard tumbling to the ground.

The chase wove through the labyrinthine market stalls. The astronauts dodged pottery stands and leapt over piles of grain sacks. Animals scattered in their path — chickens flapped their wings in alarm, and a goat, tethered to a post, bleated frantically as they sped past.

"Keep moving!" Commander Harris shouted, waving the team forward.

Klaus, with his agility and quick reflexes, helped the team navigate the obstacles. He flipped over carts and ducked under awnings, clearing the path for his comrades. His acrobatics, a blend of instinct and training, kept them one step ahead of the guards.

As the guards continued their relentless pursuit, Commander Harris made a quick decision. "We need to split up. Sophie, Ivan, take that alley. Emily, Klaus with me."

Sophie and Ivan veered into a narrow alleyway, the shadows swallowing them as they ran. They found refuge in a blacksmith's shop, the heat of the forge creating a haze in the air. The blacksmith, startled by their sudden appearance, watched in confusion as they improvised a barricade with tools and weapons.

"That should hold them for a while," Ivan said, panting.

Meanwhile, Commander Harris, Emily and Klaus continued to weave through the market, their pace unrelenting. The sounds of pursuit faded slightly as the team split, each group hoping to lose their pursuers in the maze of the Agora.

Capture of Emily

As they moved through the throng of people, Emily tripped over a loose stone. She stumbled and fell, her cloaking device slipping from her hand and clattering to the ground. Before she could retrieve it, a group of Athenian guards approached.

"Emily!" Klaus shouted, but it was too late.

Guards surged forward, seizing Emily. She struggled, but their grip was ironclad. She was quickly overpowered and dragged away, her cries lost in the noise of the market.

"Help!" she screamed, but the others were too far ahead.

"What's this?" one of the guards demanded, picking up the strange device. His eyes narrowed as he looked at Emily. "You there, where did you come from?"

Emily, trying to maintain her composure, stood up. "I am a traveler from a distant land," she said.

"A foreigner with strange tools," the guard muttered. "You will come with us for questioning."

Before Emily could protest, the guards seized her and began to drag her away. The other astronauts, watching from a distance, quickly realized they had to make a plan.

"They have arrested her. We need to get Emily back," Klaus said urgently. "We can't leave her in their hands."

"I'll use the plasma scepter," Klaus said, adjusting it to stun mode. "We can take out the guards without harming them."

"Or I'll use the medical rod to ensure no one gets seriously hurt," Klaus added.

Commander Harris shook his head. "No, later. Let's move. We can't stay here."

After a harrowing chase, the remaining astronauts reunited in a quiet back alley.

"We have to go back for Emily," Klaus said, his voice urgent.

Commander Harris nodded. "We'll get her back. But we need a plan. Sophie, can you find out where they're taking her?"

Sophie, now visible, nodded. "I'll follow them. Meet me near the large statue at the market's edge in ten minutes."

The team split up once more, determined to rescue their friend.

Sophie returned with news. "They're taking Emily to the city prison. It's heavily guarded, but we have the element of surprise."

"Good," Commander Harris said. "Klaus, you and I will handle the guards. Ivan, you create a diversion. Sophie find a way to unlock the cells."

The team moved swiftly, their actions coordinated and precise. The market chase had been chaotic, but it had also revealed their strengths. They were ready to face whatever came next.

Imprisonment

The guards led Emily to a small, dark cell in the heart of Athens. The stone walls were cold and damp, and the air was thick with the scent of mold and decay. The only light came from a small, barred window high above, casting eerie shadows across the room.

As she was thrown into the cell, Emily stumbled, landing hard on the rough stone floor. The heavy door slammed shut behind her with a resounding clang. She pushed herself up, wincing at the pain in her hands and knees.

Hours passed, each moment stretching into an eternity. The sounds of the bustling city were muted, replaced by the occasional distant cry of other prisoners and the scurrying of rats. Emily's mind raced, filled with fear and worry for her friends and the mission.

Strategic Retreat: Temple of Defense

As the sun dipped low on the horizon, casting long shadows across the ancient city of Athens, the astronauts sought refuge within the sacred halls of the Temple of Hephaestus, God of fire. Hoping the sanctity of the temple would shield them from their pursuers.

As dusk settled over Athens, the first wave of zealots descended upon the temple. Armed with spears and shields, they charged forward, their shouts echoing through the night.

The astronauts stood their ground, their resolve unwavering. With precise aim, Commander Harris and Klaus unleashed bursts of energy from the plasma scepter, stunning their assailants and driving them back.

As the zealots regrouped for another assault, Ivan sought higher ground, scaling the ancient stones of the temple's exterior. From his vantage point on the roof, he surveyed the surrounding terrain, Ivan tried to identify potential weaknesses in the attackers' approach.

As the next assault began, the astronauts braced themselves for the onslaught. With a coordinated effort, they fought off the attackers, using every tool at their disposal to maintain their defensive perimeter. The cloaking bracelet, wielded with skill by Sophie and Ivan, allowed them to confuse and ambush the zealots, turning the tide of battle in their favor.

As the last of the zealots retreated into the darkness, defeated and demoralized, the astronauts breathed a collective sigh of relief. Though weary from the ordeal, they knew they had prevailed through unity and quick thinking.

"We may be strangers in this time," Commander Harris said, his gaze sweeping over his comrades, "but as long as we stand together, we can overcome any challenge."

With newfound resolve, the astronauts prepared to face whatever trials lay ahead, knowing that their bond would carry them through.

The Interrogation

The cell door creaked open, and a group of guards entered, followed by a stern-looking man dressed in robes. His eyes were cold and calculating as he regarded Emily.

"Who are you, and where do you come from?" he demanded.

Emily took a deep breath. "I am a traveler from a distant land," she repeated, her voice steady. "I mean no harm."

The interrogator's expression hardened. "Lies will not save you," he said. He gestured to the guards, who stepped forward with cruel smiles.

They grabbed her, dragging her to a wooden chair with leather straps. Emily struggled, but their grip was too strong. They tied her down, the leather biting into her wrists and ankles.

The interrogator approached, holding a whip in his hand. "We have ways of making people talk," he said, his voice chilling. He raised the whip and brought it down across Emily's back with a sickening crack.

Emily cried out in pain, her body arching against the restraints. The whip struck again and again, each lash sending waves of agony through her. She bit her lip, refusing to give them the satisfaction of hearing her scream.

"Tell us the truth," the interrogator demanded. "Who are you, and why are you here?"

Tears streamed down Emily's face, but she remained silent. Her mind was a whirlwind of pain and fear, but she clung to the hope that her friends would come for her.

Rescue and Reunion

The team huddled together, planning their rescue operation.

"We'll need to use the cloaking bracelet to get past the guards," Sophie suggested. "It can make us invisible, but we need to be careful not to draw attention."

"We can use the plasma scepter in stun mode to incapacitate the guards quietly," Klaus added. "We don't want to kill anyone if we can avoid it."

"And the medical rod," Ivan said, holding up the device. "It can heal Emily if she's been hurt."

Commander Harris mapped out their approach. "Klaus and I will use the cloaking bracelet to get inside and locate Emily. Sophie and Ivan, you'll create a distraction outside the prison to draw some of the guards away."

As night fell, the group moved into position. Sophie and Ivan set up near the prison's entrance, preparing to create a diversion. Meanwhile, Commander Harris and Klaus activated the cloaking bracelet, their forms shimmering and then disappearing entirely.

Sophie nodded to Ivan. "Ready?"

"Ready," Ivan replied, gripping the plasma scepter.

Sophie ignited a small fire near a merchant's cart, quickly fanning the flames until they caught the attention of nearby guards. "Fire! Help, fire!" she shouted, causing a commotion.

The guards rushed to the scene, trying to extinguish the flames and shouting orders. In the chaos, Ivan used the plasma scepter to stun a few guards quietly, ensuring they wouldn't return to the prison anytime soon.

Using the cloaking bracelet, Commander Harris and Klaus slipped through the gates, moving silently through the prison corridors. They found Emily's cell quickly – she was bound, her face pale but resolute.

Commander Harris used the plasma scepter to disable the cell's lock.

As the interrogation continued, the door burst open. The guards turned, only to be struck down by blasts from the plasma scepter in stun mode. Commander Harris and Klaus charged in, disarming the remaining guards.

Klaus deactivated the cloaking device, revealing their presence. "Emily, we're here."

Emily looked up, relief flooding her eyes. "Thank goodness. I didn't know how much longer I could hold out."

Klaus rushed to Emily's side, quickly untied her and used the medical rod to heal her wounds. The pain subsided, replaced by a soothing warmth. "Emily, are you okay?" Klaus asked, her eyes filled with concern.

Emily, her voice hoarse, nodded. "I'm fine. Let's get out of here."

"We need to move, now," Commander Harris urged.

They reactivated the cloaking bracelet, this time cloaking all three of them as they moved stealthily back through the prison. The distraction outside had drawn most of the guards away, making their escape easier.

As they fled through the streets of Athens, Emily leaned on Klaus for support, her body still trembling from the ordeal. Now she has already felt protected twice by Klaus in her primal instinct. The first time she had experienced this was when she was knocked out by the plasma scepter as the first artifact in the hidden chamber of the Martian pyramid and was caught in Klaus' arms. Will there be a third time soon? Or as Klaus has initially cited the common saying during her lecture on volcanoes and impact craters:"three times are charming!" "There you go again, Emily, you have fallen hopelessly in love", Emily said to herself.

Outside, the group reunited, the night still dark and filled with the sounds of distant chaos. They quickly moved away from the prison, heading towards the outskirts of the city.

"We did it," Ivan said, a grin spreading across his face.

Emily, still a bit shaken but smiling, replied, "Thanks to all of you. I wouldn't have made it without your help."

Finding Socrates

With Emily safely back with the group, they quickly made their way through the city, avoiding patrols and blending in with the crowds. They eventually reached the outskirts of the Agora, where they found a small gathering of people listening to a man speak.

"There he is," Ivan said, pointing to a figure in simple robes. "Socrates."

The group approached cautiously, not wanting to disrupt the gathering. As they drew closer, they could hear Socrates' voice, deep and resonant, asking probing questions and engaging his audience in philosophical debate.

"Socrates," Commander Harris called out, drawing the philosopher's attention.

Socrates turned to face them, his eyes twinkling with curiosity. "Ah, more travelers! What brings you to Athens, and why do you seek me?"

"We come from a distant land and time," Emily said, stepping forward. "We seek your wisdom."

Socrates studied them for a moment before smiling. "Wisdom, you say? It is a rare and precious thing. Come, sit with me, and let us talk."

The astronauts sat down with Socrates, sharing their experiences and the purpose of their journey. Socrates listened intently, occasionally asking questions that challenged their assumptions and made them think more deeply about their mission.

A Philosophical Encounter

The Discussion Begins

The astronauts sat down on stone benches. Socrates looked at each of them, his eyes filled with curiosity and warmth. "What brings you to me, strangers? What do you seek?"

Commander Harris started to speak:"We seek to understand the nature of justice, the meaning of virtue, and the essence of the human soul. Your teachings have inspired generations, and we hope to gain insight into these timeless questions."

Socrates nodded:"Wise inquiries, indeed. Let us embark on a journey of intellectual exploration together. But first, let us acknowledge the limits of our knowledge. For true wisdom begins with the recognition of one's own ignorance."

Ivan butted in:"How do we reconcile the pursuit of virtue with the complexities of human nature? Is it possible to attain true goodness in a world filled with moral ambiguity?"

Socrates answered readily:"A profound question, my friend. Virtue, I believe, lies not in the absence of wrongdoing, but in the conscious pursuit of excellence. It is a journey of self-discovery, guided by reason and tempered by humility."

Now Emily brought up her questions:"Socrates, how do we cultivate wisdom in a world inundated with information? In an age of technological advancement, how do we discern truth from falsehood?

Socrates smiled knowingly:"The pursuit of wisdom requires discipline and discernment. We must learn to question our assumptions, to challenge our beliefs, and to seek knowledge with an open mind. For it is only through rigorous inquiry that we may hope to uncover the truths that lie beyond the veil of ignorance."

Klaus, with the benefits of his classical education, delved even deeper into the complex philosophical discussion:"Socrates, how do we navigate the complexities of human relationships? How do we cultivate friendship and foster goodwill in a world torn apart by strife and division?"

Socrates was delighted with Klaus's question:"Friendship, my young friend, is a sacred bond — a union of souls bound by mutual respect, trust, and goodwill. It is through genuine human connection that we find solace in times of hardship, joy in times of celebration, and meaning in the shared experience of life."

The Meaning of Life

Commander Harris spoke up, his voice steady. "We seek to understand the meaning of life. How do we find meaning in a universe that seems indifferent to our existence? We have traveled far and wide, through time and space, searching for answers."

Socrates smiled. "Ah, the meaning of life, my dear friend, a question as old as time itself. It is a question that has puzzled philosophers for millennia. Some believe it lies in the pursuit of pleasure, others in the pursuit of knowledge. But I believe that the true meaning is to be found in the pursuit of virtue, self-knowledge and wisdom. Tell me, what have you learned so far on your journey?"

Sophie leaned forward. "We have learned that life is precious and fragile. We have seen civilizations rise and fall, and we have witnessed acts of great kindness and terrible cruelty. But we still do not fully grasp the purpose of our existence."

Socrates nodded. "Life's purpose is not something easily defined. It is a tapestry woven from our experiences, actions, and beliefs. Each thread, each moment, contributes to the whole."

Klaus, the team's science officer, leaned in. "But how do we find this path of virtue and wisdom in a world filled with so much uncertainty and conflict?"

Socrates smiled gently. "Uncertainty and conflict are part of the human experience. They challenge us, test our resolve, and help us grow. The key is to remain true to oneself, to question assumptions, and to seek truth in all things. Engage in dialogue, learn from others, and strive to be the best version of yourself."

Ivan asked, "But Socrates, in our time, we face challenges that seem insurmountable. How can we apply your teachings to overcome them?"

Socrates nodded, understanding the gravity of the question. "By focusing on what you can control. Your thoughts, actions, and choices. Lead by example, inspire others with your integrity and wisdom. Remember that every great change often begins with a single step, a single person willing to question and strive for better."

Commander Harris looked around at his team, then back at Socrates. "Thank you, Socrates. Your words give us strength and clarity. We will carry your wisdom with us as we continue our journey."

Socrates placed a hand on Commander Harris' shoulder. "Remember that true wisdom comes from knowing yourself and understanding that you know very little. Keep questioning, keep searching, and you will find your way. " He looked at everyone: "May you find what you are looking for, travelers. And don't forget that an unexamined life is not worth living."

As the conversation came to a close, the astronauts felt a deep sense of peace and purpose. They knew their journey was far from over, but with the wisdom of Socrates to guide them, they felt ready to face whatever challenges lay ahead.

With gratitude, they bid farewell to the great philosopher, promising to carry his teachings into the future. As they activated their device and disappeared from ancient Athens, they felt a renewed sense of purpose and a deeper understanding of the meaning of life.

Chapter 26: The Longevity Pod

The Martian pyramid stood silent and imposing under the thin Martian atmosphere, its angular sides reflecting the faint light from the distant sun. After their various explorations through time and history, the astronauts felt a sense of duty to continue uncovering the secrets of the pyramid. As the five remaining astronauts continued their exploration of the Martian pyramid, their discoveries grew ever more astounding. Each new chamber unveiled relics and artifacts that painted a richer picture of the A'kara civilization's advanced knowledge and capabilities. Each discovery had brought them closer to understanding, and they were certain that many more secrets lay within the walls. Their search led them deeper into the pyramid, towards a chamber that would challenge their understanding of life and mortality.

Emily was the first to notice the peculiar inscriptions on a hidden door at the end of a dimly lit corridor. The symbols were unlike any they had seen before, more intricate and elaborate, hinting at a significant chamber beyond.

"Everyone, look at this," Emily called out, tracing her fingers over the carvings.

Ivan examined the symbols closely. "These are different. They seem to depict some kind of advanced technology."

Using their portable translation device, which Wei has left, they were able to decipher the inscriptions. "They speak of 'renewal' and 'preservation'. This could be somehow related to life extension or immortality," Emily said.

Excited and cautious, the team worked together to open the door, revealing a vast chamber filled with a soft, ambient glow. At the center of the room stood a large, ornate pod, unlike anything they had encountered so far.

It was crafted from a smooth, metallic material, inscribed with the same intricate symbols. Its design was elegant, exuding an aura of wisdom. Surrounding the pod were various panels and consoles with unknown but captivating glyphs on their surfaces.

"This could be a major breakthrough. If the inscriptions are correct, this might be a longevity regeneration or hibernation pod," Commander Harris presumed.

Sophie examined the panels. "It's extraordinary. The technology here seems light-years ahead of ours. The A'kara truly mastered the science of life."

Klaus nodded. "We need to understand how it works. This could provide insights into their biological advancements."

They found a lock that seemed to fit the Cosmic Key they had received from the Celestial Council. After Commander Harris inserted the key into the lock, the pod opened with a roar.

With a mixture of excitement and trepidation, the team decided to activate the pod. Emily carefully manipulated the controls, her expertise in engineering proving invaluable. The pod hummed to life, its surfaces glowing with a soft, pulsing light.

"According to the symbols, the pod is designed to induce a state of hibernation and promote cellular regeneration," Emily explained.

Commander Harris, being the oldest member of the crew, volunteered to test the pod. "If this works, it could be a game-changer for long-term space travel and even life extension on Earth. I'll do it. If things go wrong, Emily will be in charge as the First Officer in command. And Ivan, you are the Second Officer in command and give full support to Emily. I am convinced that you both will lead this mission to success."

Emily and Ivan nodded in concerted agreement.

Klaus encouraged Commander Harris saying:"Alright, go for it! You definitely deserve it. I will envy you in the end for sure!"

The team prepped Commander Harris for the procedure, monitoring his vital signs and ensuring all safety protocols were in place. As he lay inside the pod, its lid closed with a gentle hiss, enveloping him in a cocoon of light.

Inside the pod, Commander Harris felt a wave of warmth and tranquility wash over him. The pod's interior was designed for comfort, with a soft, almost breathable material conforming to his body. He could feel a gentle pulsation, like a heartbeat, resonating through the pod, syncing with his own.

Outside, the team monitored the readouts on the panels. The glyphs indicated that the pod was functioning correctly, initiating the hibernation and regeneration process.

Ivan watched intently. "His vitals are stable. The pod's systems are engaging with his cellular structure. It's remarkable."

For several hours, the team observed as the pod worked its magic. The readings indicated a significant decrease in metabolic activity, consistent with a deep hibernation state. Simultaneously, the regeneration sequences showed signs of enhanced cellular repair and rejuvenation.

After a set duration, the pod's cycle completed, and the lid slowly opened. Commander Harris emerged, looking visibly refreshed and energized. His crewmates rushed to his side, eager to hear about his experience.

"How do you feel, Commander?" Ivan asked, scanning him with a medical device.

Commander Harris was silent and appeared impassive. Ivan turned to the commander again and shook him gently.

As this did not show any effect, he turned to him again, shook him harder and kept saying, "Commander? — Commander? — John?"

There was still no reaction. The crew members were concerned that their commander was feeling numb still and he was lying there apathetically. Ivan was convinced of his readings and said to the others:"You sometimes get that after long anesthesia during surgeries. This is a kind of hangover. There is an antidote such as flumazenil for tranquilizers like benzodiazepines, but I only have the brute method available here."

Then Ivan turned back to the commander and tried shaking him again, but this time he was rubbing his fist on the commander's sternum to inflict pain.

Suddenly the commander opened his eyes and said:"Ouch!"

"Welcome back to Mars!", Ivan said smiling.

After a short while, Commander Harris also smiled, a look of astonishment in his eyes. "Incredible. I feel like I've had the best rest of my life. There's a sense of rejuvenation, as if my body's been repaired from within."

Ivan checked the medical readouts. "Your vitals are better than before. It's as if you've undergone a cellular reset."

Klaus examined the pod. "The A'kara's technology is beyond our wildest dreams. This device could revolutionize medicine."

The discovery of the longevity regeneration pod opened up new possibilities for the astronauts. They realized that the A'kara's mastery over life and longevity was far more advanced than they had anticipated.

Sophie summarized their thoughts. "We need to document every detail of this technology. If we can understand how it works, it could lead to breakthroughs in our scientific fields."

Commander Harris nodded. "We should proceed with caution, though. We need to ensure we fully understand the implications and potential side effects. But this… this is a gift from the A'kara. A chance to push the boundaries of human capability."

As the team continued their exploration, they knew that the knowledge they had gained from the A'kara was only the beginning. The secrets of the ancient Martian civilization held the potential to transform humanity's future, offering new horizons in longevity, space travel, and the understanding of life itself.

With renewed determination, the astronauts pressed on, ready to unlock more of the A'kara's mysteries and share their discoveries with the world. The legacy of the A'kara civilization was now intertwined with their own, a testament to the enduring spirit of exploration and the quest for knowledge.

Chapter 27: A Divergent Path

The Martian dawn cast a faint, ethereal glow through the entrance of the pyramid, painting the chamber walls with soft hues of orange and red. The discovery of the gateway had presented the astronauts with a profound choice: to return to Earth with the collected knowledge in a shortcut without a space flight of several months or to stay and find out more about the A'kara civilization. The air was thick with unspoken tension as the team gathered to discuss their next steps.

The Rift Emerges

The team assembled in the central chamber, the holographic images of the Celestial Council still fresh in their minds. At the other end was the gateway through which Wei had already passed.

Commander Harris looked at his team, his voice steady but his eyes betraying the weight of their decision. "We've come a long way, and we've uncovered incredible knowledge. The gateway is our way back to Earth. But I need to know where each of you stands."

Sophie glanced at Ivan, her expression conflicted. She took a deep breath, her resolve firming as she stepped forward. "I've made my decision. I'm staying."

The room fell silent. Ivan looked at Sophie, a mixture of surprise and concern in his eyes. "Sophie, what are you talking about? We need to go back and share what we've found."

Sophie shook her head. "We've only scratched the surface of the A'kara's knowledge. There's so much more to discover here, and I can't leave without understanding it fully. This is the opportunity of a lifetime."

Ivan's Dilemma

Ivan felt a pang of anguish. He had grown close to Sophie during their time on Mars, their shared experiences forging a bond that went beyond their mission. Her decision to stay tore at his heart, but he understood her passion for discovery.

Ivan looked at Sophie with a worried expression:"Sophie, if you stay, what happens to us? To everything we've built together?"

Sophie's eyes softened, but her determination remained. "Ivan, I can't let this chance slip away. The A'kara's secrets could change everything we know about the universe, about our place in it. I need to stay and learn."

Ivan looked at the gateway, then back at Sophie. He took her hands in his, his voice filled with a mixture of love and resignation. "Then I'll stay with you. I can't leave you here alone."

Sophie squeezed his hands, her eyes glistening with gratitude. "Thank you, Ivan. Together, we can find out the other secrets about the A'ka-ra."

The rest of the team exchanged glances, processing the gravity of Sophie and Ivan's decision. Emily stepped forward, her expression one of understanding and respect.

Emily gave Sophie a determined look and shortly afterwards turned to Ivan:"We respect your decision, Sophie. And Ivan, your loyalty is admirable."

Commander Harris nodded. "We need to think about the bigger picture. What we've learned here is invaluable. But we can't force you to return if you believe your place is here."

Klaus said with a conciliatory look: "Emily and I will make sure the information we have reaches Earth safely. But if you find more, find a way to communicate it to us."

Preparing for Departure

The team spent the next few hours preparing for the separation. Sophie and Ivan gathered supplies and equipment, ensuring they had everything they needed to continue their exploration of the pyramid. The others prepared the data they had collected, securing it for the journey back to Earth.

Emily approached Sophie, her eyes filled with a mixture of admiration and concern. "You're brave, Sophie. I hope you find what you're looking for."

Sophie smiled, appreciating the sentiment. "Thank you, Emily. I hope our paths cross again."

The Final Farewell

As the moment of departure approached, the team gathered one last time in front of the gateway. The shimmering archway loomed behind them, a symbol of both separation and hope.

Commander Harris:"Sophie, Ivan, you both have been incredible teammates. I wish you all the best."

Ivan nodded, his grip firm on Sophie's hand. "And we'll carry the mission forward here. We'll keep in touch."

Emily stepped forward, her voice tinged with emotion. "Take care of each other. And remember, you're not alone. We're all part of this mission, no matter where we are."

With final hugs and handshakes, the team bid farewell. Sophie and Ivan watched as their friends stepped through the gateway, the shimmering light enveloping them before they vanished from sight.

And now a decimated crew returned to Earth, consisting of only three astronauts.

Thanks to the cosmic key, however, Commander Harris, Emily and Klaus were spared a detour via a sentinel test through several chambers, which Wei had to pass beforehand.

The atmosphere was a little spooky. At the other far end of the gateway, the shape of an Egyptian pyramid on Earth emerged from the Martian pyramid.

A short time later, the three of them found themselves in the Egyptian desert, where they were happily welcomed by Wei and a team of scientists, medical doctors and security personnel.

Commander Harris stepped out, his body trembling as the familiar gravity of Earth took hold. The transition from Mars to Earth was disorienting, a rush of sensations flooding his mind. He found himself on the soil where his journey had begun, surrounded by a team of scientists and officials eager to debrief him and the others.

Lead Scientist:"Welcome back, Commander Harris. Your journey was a success. We've received all your preliminary data. How are you feeling?"

Commander Harris replied:"A bit overwhelmed, but relieved. There's so much to share."

Despite the exertions on Mars, a rehabilitation program was now required for several weeks, as the cardiovascular performance had to be carefully adapted to the conditions on Earth due to the almost 1/3 reduction in gravity on Mars compared to Earth. However, the shortcut through the gateway spared them a return flight in space lasting several months, so that they benefited enormously both physically and mentally.

The days (and not sols anymore) that followed were a whirlwind of activity. The astronauts spent countless hours in debriefing sessions, sharing the findings of the A'kara civilization, the trials they had faced, and the incredible legacy they had uncovered. Their contributions were invaluable, sparking a renewed interest in space exploration and the potential for human colonization of Mars.

A New Beginning

Sophie and Ivan stood in the now quiet chamber, the weight of their decision settling over them. They were alone on an alien world, but they were together, driven by a shared purpose.

Sophie looked at Ivan, her eyes filled with determination. "We have a lot of work to do. The A'kara's secrets won't uncover themselves."

Ivan nodded, a sense of peace and resolve filling him. "Let's get started. We have a civilization to discover."

Hand in hand, they turned away from the gateway and ventured deeper into the pyramid, ready to face whatever challenges lay ahead. Their journey had taken an unexpected turn, but together, they were prepared to unlock the mysteries of the A'kara and carry their legacy forward.

Epilogue: A New Dawn on Mars — and on Earth

The Martian sun rose slowly over the horizon, casting a warm, amber glow across the vast, rocky landscape. The ancient pyramid stood as a silent sentinel, its smooth, reddish stones imbued with the wisdom and secrets of the A'kara civilization. Inside the pyramid, life had taken on a new meaning for Sophie and Ivan, who had chosen to stay behind and delve deeper into the mysteries of Mars.

A New Chapter for Sophie and Ivan

Months had passed since the team had departed, leaving Sophie and Ivan alone to continue their exploration. The knowledge they had uncovered and the bond they had forged made them inseparable. Every day brought new discoveries, and every night, they gazed at the stars, dreaming of the future they were building together on this alien world.

Sophie gently cradled her newborn baby, the first human born on Mars. The child, a symbol of hope and a bridge between two worlds, had brought an unprecedented sense of purpose and joy to their lives.

Sophie turned happily to Ivan:"Look, Ivan. Our little one is so perfect. The first Martian-born human being."

Ivan smiled, his eyes filled with love and pride. "Our legacy, Sophie. A symbol of the bond between Earth and Mars."

Life on Mars

Life on Mars had its challenges, but Sophie and Ivan faced them with unwavering determination. They had established a small but functional habitat within the pyramid, using the technology and resources left behind by their teammates. Solar panels provided power, and a hydroponic garden supplied fresh food.

They had also continued their research, uncovering more about the A'kara and their advanced understanding of the universe. The pyramid's walls seemed to resonate with their presence, as if the ancient civilization itself was welcoming and guiding them.

Sophie:"The A'kara's legacy is becoming clearer. Their knowledge of cosmic energies and their understanding of life and immortality are beyond anything we could have imagined."

Ivan:"And our child will grow up with this legacy, Sophie. We're creating a new chapter in human history."

Life on Earth

On Earth, the return of Commander Harris, Emily and Klaus and their reunion with Wei triggered a revolution in scientific thinking and research. They had shared their findings, inspiring a new wave of interest in space exploration and the potential for human colonization of Mars.

Wei's Destiny

The Weight of Knowledge

Despite the professional accolades and the excitement surrounding their discoveries, Wei felt an emptiness within. The bonds she had formed with her fellow astronauts on Mars had left an indelible mark on her heart, and she missed them deeply.

She returned to her apartment in Beijing, the city bustling with life, a stark contrast to the sterile environment of the ivory tower of mission control or to the silent expanse of Mars. Her apartment felt both comforting and strange, a reminder of the life she had left behind.

Reconnecting with Family

One of the first things Wei did was reconnect with her family. Her parents had been anxiously awaiting her return, their relief palpable when they finally embraced her.

Wei's Mother:"Wei, we were so worried about you. You've been so brave."

Wei's Father:"You've done amazing things, Wei."

Wei replied:"I missed you both so much. Mars was incredible, but it's good to be home."

They spent hours talking, Wei sharing her experiences and her parents listening with awe. They were proud of her accomplishments but also concerned about the toll the mission had taken on her.

As Wei settled back into her life on Earth, she struggled to find a balance between her professional responsibilities and her personal needs. The scientific community was abuzz with the findings from Mars, and she was constantly in demand for interviews, lectures, and conferences. But amidst the chaos, Wei yearned for peace and normality. She reconnected with old friends, seeking solace in familiar faces and the simple pleasures of everyday life.

A friend from school talked to her:"It's like you've been to another world, Wei. How do you even begin to describe it?"

Wei replied:"It's hard to put into words. It was beautiful and challenging, but I'm glad to be back."

As she navigated her new reality, Wei found herself drawn to someone unexpected — Dr. Michael Chen, a fellow scientist who had been part of the team analyzing the data from Mars. Michael was kind, intelligent, and shared her passion for exploration.

They spent long hours discussing their work, their dreams, and their experiences. Michael was fascinated by Wei's stories from Mars, and she found comfort in his understanding and support.

Michael addressed her coquettishly:"You've been through so much, Wei. I admire your strength."

Wei replied with a smile:"Thank you, Michael. It's been a journey, but I feel like I've finally found my place."

Their friendship blossomed into a romance, and Wei felt a new sense of happiness and fulfillment. Michael helped her see the beauty in the present, and together they dreamed of the future.

Moving Forward

With Michael by her side, Wei began to look forward, rather than

dwelling on the past. They talked about future missions, the potential for returning to Mars, and even the possibility of starting a family someday.

Wei explained to Michael:"Mars will always be a part of me, but I'm excited for what's to come."

Michael added:"And whatever the future holds, we'll face it together."

A New Dawn

Wei continued to work tirelessly to share the legacy of the A'kara civilization. She wrote papers, gave talks, and collaborated with scientists around the world to further understand and disseminate the knowledge they had uncovered.

Her efforts were not just about scientific discovery, but also about bridging the gap between worlds — between Earth and Mars, and between the past and the future.

As the years passed, Wei found a sense of balance and peace. She and Michael built a life together, grounded in love and mutual respect. They continued their work, driven by the knowledge that they were part of something greater than themselves.

One evening, as the sun set over Beijing, Wei stood on her balcony, looking up at the night sky. The stars twinkled brightly, and she felt a deep connection to the universe.

Wei spoke to Michael: "We've only just begun to explore. There's so much more out there."

Michael joined her, wrapping his arms around her. "And we'll explore it together, Wei."

With a smile, Wei turned to him, feeling a sense of contentment and hope. They had both found their place in the world, and the legacy of the A'kara would continue to inspire them and future generations.

As they stood together, gazing at the stars, Wei knew that her journey was far from over. The possibilities were endless, and she was ready to face whatever came next, hand in hand with the man she loved.

Commander Harris

Return to Earth as a Widower

After Commander Harris had returned to Earth, completed the briefings and received recognition, he returned to his home in Houston, Texas. He was overcome with a deep sense of loneliness. He had lost his wife Rachel in a traffic accident a year before the Mars mission. The house was full of memories of Rachel - her laughter, her warmth and the life they had built together. He wandered through the rooms, touching the mementos of their life together, feeling simultaneously comforted and heartbroken. Her absence was a constant ache, a void that even the wonders of Mars could not fill.

Commander Harris spoke to the souvenir photo:"Rachel, I wish you could have seen Mars. It was everything we dreamed of and more."

Support from Friends and Colleagues

Commander Harris's close friends and colleagues rallied around him, offering support and companionship. His best friend, Mark Thompson, who had been his confidant since their days in the Air Force, was a constant presence.

Mark said:"It's good to have you back, John. We've missed you. How are you holding up?"

Commander Harris:"It's been tough, Mark. Coming back to an empty house… it's harder than I thought it would be."

Mark nodded, understanding the weight of John's grief. "We're here for you, buddy. Anytime you need us."

Commander Harris threw himself into his work, accepting a senior position at the space agency as Director of Mars Research and Exploration. His experience on Mars made him an invaluable asset, and he was determined to ensure that the mission's legacy continued.

He spent long hours in the lab and at meetings, working on new strategies for future Mars missions and mentoring young astronauts. This work gave him a sense of fulfillment and a way to process his grief.

Dr. Sarah Mitchell, one of his mentees, admired his dedication and often sought his guidance.

Sarah praised him:"Commander Harris, your insights are invaluable. You've inspired us all."

Commander Harris replied, somewhat embarrassed:"Thank you, Sarah. It's important to keep pushing the boundaries of what we know. That's what Rachel always believed in."

A Chance Encounter

One evening, while attending a charity event for families of astronauts, John met Dr. Laura Bennett, a psychologist who specialized in helping astronauts and their families cope with the psychological challenges of space travel. Laura Bennett lived separately from her partner and was a single mother of two children. She had heard about Commander Harris's loss and approached him with a warm smile.

Laura Bennett introduced herself to the commander:"Commander Harris, I'm Laura Bennett. I've read all about your mission. It's an honor to meet you."

Commander Harris:"The honor is mine, Dr. Bennett. Please, call me John."

Their conversation flowed easily, and Commander Harris found himself opening up to Laura Bennett in a way he hadn't with anyone since Rachel's death. Laura Bennett's empathy and understanding provided him with a sense of comfort he hadn't felt in a long time.

As the evening wore on, they indulged in a dance together to the calm jazz music in the background. They enjoyed their time together and Commander Harris's loneliness seemed to be forgotten for a moment.

A Blossoming Friendship

Over the following months, John and Laura developed a close friendship. They often met for coffee, discussing their work, their lives, and their shared passion for space exploration. Laura's presence became a source of solace and healing for John.

On one day, Laura said to John: "You've been through so much, John. It's okay to let yourself grieve."

John replied, nodding: "Thank you, Laura. Your support means more to me than I can say."

As their bond grew stronger, John began to feel the first stirrings of hope and happiness. He realized that while Rachel's memory would always be a part of him, he didn't have to face the future alone.

With Laura's encouragement, John began to embrace life outside of work. They attended social events together, went on hiking trips, and shared quiet evenings watching the stars — activities that brought back John's sense of wonder and joy.

One evening, as they sat on a hill overlooking the city, Laura turned to John with a gentle smile.

Laura said to John directly:"John, I know you'll always love Rachel. She was an incredible person. But I want you to know that I'm here for you, whatever the future holds."

John answered her gratefully: "Thank you, Laura. I've been afraid to move forward, but you've shown me that it's possible. I'm grateful for you every day."

John continued to excel in his role at the space agency, but now he had a renewed sense of purpose. He and Laura grew closer, their relationship evolving from friendship to something deeper. With Laura by his side, John felt ready to face whatever challenges and adventures lay ahead.

Their relationship blossomed, and John found himself envisioning a future filled with new possibilities. He and Laura talked about their dreams, both personal and professional, and how they could support each other in achieving them.

Legacy of the A'kara

John remained dedicated to the legacy of the A'kara civilization. He wrote extensively about their discoveries, gave public lectures, and worked tirelessly to inspire future generations of explorers.

Excerpt from John's Speech:"The A'kara taught us that the universe is vast and full of wonders. Our journey to Mars was just the beginning. We must continue to explore, to learn, and to push the boundaries of human knowledge."

As the years passed, John and Laura's relationship grew stronger. They faced life's challenges together, their bond deepening with each passing day. Laura's children, Jordan and Mia, embraced John as part of their family, finding joy in the new life they were building.

On a warm spring day, surrounded by friends and loved ones, John and Laura stood together and exchanged vows, committing to a future filled with love, exploration, and discovery.

Laura stated:"John, you've shown me the strength to move forward and the courage to dream. I'm honored to walk this path with you."

John replied:"Laura, you've brought light back into my life. Together, we'll face whatever comes, and we'll make the most of every moment."

With Laura's support, John continued to inspire and lead, both at space agency and in his personal life. He knew that Rachel would always be a part of him, but he had found a new partner to share his journey.

As they stood together, watching the sun set over the horizon, John felt a sense of peace and fulfillment. He had come a long way from the lonely, grief-stricken man who had returned from Mars. With Laura, her children, and his work, he had found a new beginning.

And as he gazed at the stars, he knew that the future was filled with endless possibilities, a testament to the resilience of the human spirit and the enduring power of love.

Klaus's Contribution to Transhumanism

Klaus's interest in genetics and DNA was not merely academic; it was deeply rooted in his belief in transhumanism. This philosophical movement advocates for the use of technology to enhance human physical and cognitive abilities, pushing the boundaries of what it means to be human. After returning from the Martian expedition, Klaus saw an opportunity to contribute to this vision in meaningful ways. Upon his return to Earth, Klaus transformed his state-of-the-art laboratory into a hub for transhumanist research. It was a place where cutting-edge technology met bold, forward-thinking ideas. His lab now housed advanced gene-editing tools, sophisticated biometric sensors, and AI-driven analysis systems, all designed to explore and enhance human capabilities.

Defining the Research Goals

Klaus set ambitious research goals that aligned with the core tenets of transhumanism:

1. Enhanced Physical Resilience: To make humans more resistant to diseases, aging, and extreme environments.

2. Cognitive Enhancement: To boost mental faculties, including memory, learning speed, and problem-solving abilities.

3. Sensory Augmentation: To extend human senses beyond their natural limits, incorporating abilities such as night vision and heightened sensitivity to electromagnetic fields.

Experimentation and Innovation

Klaus's approach was systematic and rigorous. He began by focusing on enhancing physical resilience, inspired by the extremophiles he had studied on Mars. Extremophiles are organisms that have adapted to extreme environmental conditions. His first major project was to integrate genes from these resilient organisms into the human genome.

1. Gene Integration:

Klaus isolated specific genes from extremophiles, such as tardigrades and Deinococcus radiodurans, which are known for their incredible resilience to radiation and extreme conditions. Using CRISPR-Cas9, the "genetic scissors", he successfully inserted these genes into human stem cells.

2. Cell Culturing and Testing:

The modified cells were cultured in a controlled environment. Klaus subjected them to various stress tests, including radiation exposure and extreme temperature fluctuations. The results were promising—these cells showed a significant increase in resilience compared to unmodified cells.

3. Clinical Trials:

Klaus then moved on to conducting clinical trials with volunteers. These trials were meticulously designed and closely monitored to ensure the safety and efficacy of the genetic modifications. Volunteers reported improved resistance to common ailments and quicker recovery times.

Cognitive Enhancement

Next, Klaus turned his attention to cognitive enhancement. He explored the potential of nootropics ("smart drugs") and neural interface technologies to boost brain function. By integrating AI-driven neurofeedback systems, he aimed to create a seamless interface between the human brain and digital technologies.

1. Neuroplasticity Stimulation:

Klaus developed protocols to stimulate neuroplasticity, the brain's ability to reorganize itself. Through a combination of genetic modifications and targeted brain stimulation, volunteers showed significant improvements in learning speed and memory retention.

2. AI-Enhanced Learning:

Using AI algorithms, Klaus created personalized learning programs that adapted to each individual's cognitive profile. This approach not only accelerated learning but also helped identify and address cognitive weaknesses.

Sensory Augmentation

Klaus's final goal was to extend human sensory capabilities. Inspired by animals with extraordinary senses, he worked on integrating these abilities into the human sensory system.

1. Night Vision:

By integrating genes responsible for the enhanced night vision of certain animals, Klaus was able to give volunteers the ability to see clearly in low-light conditions.

2. Electromagnetic Sensitivity:

Another breakthrough was the integration of genes that allowed humans to detect electromagnetic fields. This ability, common in sharks and certain birds, opened up new possibilities for navigation and environmental awareness.

Ethical Considerations

Throughout his research, Klaus was acutely aware of the ethical implications of his work. He believed that transhumanism should not only enhance human abilities but also be accessible and equitable. He engaged in ongoing dialogues with ethicists, policymakers, and the public to ensure that his research adhered to ethical standards and considered the broader societal impacts.

Impact and Legacy

Klaus's work in transhumanism garnered significant attention and sparked widespread interest and debate. His research was published in leading scientific journals, and he became a prominent figure in the transhumanist community. His contributions not only advanced the field of genetic engineering but also brought the vision of transhumanism closer to reality.

Klaus's innovative approach to enhancing human capabilities showcased the potential of science and technology to push the boundaries of human potential. His legacy was one of bold experimentation, ethical responsibility, and an unwavering belief in the transformative power of science. As humanity looked to the future, Klaus's work served as a beacon of what could be achieved through ingenuity and determination.

The Deep Bond Between Emily and Klaus

The astronauts had returned to Earth, their mission complete, but their lives forever changed.

Emily was happy about Klaus' constant presence. Their shared passion for unraveling mysteries had blossomed into something deeper — a connection forged amidst the ancient hieroglyphs of Mars.

Klaus, the pragmatic biologist and chemist, had once believed that equations held all the answers. But Emily had shown him that love defied logic. Emily and Klaus had found solace in each other, their shared experiences on Mars strengthening their bond. They had decided to marry, a celebration of life and love amidst the backdrop of their incredible journey.

On their wedding day, as they stood before friends and colleagues, Emily's thoughts turned to Sophie and Ivan. "I hope they're watching," she whispered to Klaus. "I hope they know how much we miss them."

Klaus nodded, his hand tightening around hers. "They're part of this, Emily. Their choice has paved the way for all of us. Their child is a legend already." As he said this, he winked mischievously at Emily.

They married in a small ceremony, surrounded by their fellow astronauts and the memories of Mars.

Their home became a blend of scientific instruments and cozy corners — a laboratory where Emily analyzed Martian soil samples and a kitchen where Klaus brewed his famous coffee.

And then came the news — their own cosmic miracle. Emily's laughter filled their tiny apartment as she held up the ultrasound image. Emily was pregnant. Klaus's eyes widened, and he stumbled over his words, overwhelmed by the idea of becoming a father. The Martian echoes whispered secrets to their unborn child, weaving tales of ancient civilizations and interstellar gateways.

As Emily's belly grew, so did their love. Klaus read bedtime stories to the baby, spinning tales of brave astronauts and distant planets. Emily hummed melodies she'd heard on Mars, and the baby kicked in response. They chose a name together — Aria — a nod to the cosmic symphony that had brought them together.

When Aria was born, she had Klaus's analytical mind and Emily's insatiable curiosity. Her eyes held the same wonder as they gazed at the stars. The family of three would sit on their rooftop, wrapped in blankets, pointing out constellations. Aria's tiny finger traced the imaginary lines connecting Orion's Belt, and Klaus whispered, "Maybe there are other civilizations out there, waiting to be discovered."

Emily leaned against him, her head on his shoulder. "Or maybe," she said, "we're the echoes of something greater — a love story written across time and space."

And so, in the quiet moments between diaper changes and midnight feedings, Emily and Klaus dreamed of returning to Mars. Aria would grow up hearing tales of the five-sided pyramid, the alien stone face, and the gateway that bridged worlds. She'd inherit their passion for exploration, their love for the unknown. Aria's laughter echoed through their home, and Klaus taught her to balance equations while Emily painted Martian landscapes. They hung a photograph of the pyramid above the fireplace — a reminder of their shared adventure and the love that had bloomed on Mars. And so, in the warmth of their family, Emily and Klaus found their greatest discovery — their own little universe, bound by love, curiosity, and the echoes of the red horizon of another world.

A Bright Future

Back on Mars, Sophie and Ivan watched the recorded messages from their friends on Earth. The wedding ceremony had brought tears to Sophie's eyes, while Ivan felt a deep sense of connection to the world they had left behind.

Sophie said with a sob:"They're so happy, Ivan. Emily and Klaus are married and they will soon become parents too. And look at all the support they're receiving for continued exploration."

Ivan comforted Sophie:"Don't be sad. Even if we couldn't create a wedding ceremony with people around us, look what we got instead. We've started something amazing, Sophie. Our child's generation will see a united effort to understand the universe."

As the Martian sun set, casting long shadows across the pyramid, Sophie and Ivan looked at each other, their baby nestled between them. They had made a bold choice to stay, and in doing so, they had become pioneers of a new frontier.

Sophie said resolutely:"This is just the beginning, Ivan. Our child's future is bright, filled with the promise of discovery and the legacy of the A'kara."

Ivan reaffirmed what Sophie had said:"Together, we'll continue to uncover the secrets of Mars and beyond. Our journey is far from over."

A Message to Future Generations

In their final message to Earth, Sophie and Ivan expressed their hopes and dreams for the future of human exploration and the new world they were building on Mars.

Sophie started to speak the message:"To our friends and colleagues on Earth, we want you to know that we're thriving here. Our child is healthy and strong, and we're continuing our research. The A'kara's legacy is profound, we're committed to uncovering its mysteries."

Ivan concluded:"We hope our story inspires future generations to reach for the stars. Mars is just the beginning. Together, we can explore the cosmos and unlock the secrets of the universe."

As their message was transmitted back to Earth, Sophie and Ivan looked out at the Martian landscape, filled with hope and anticipation for the future. They had chosen to stay behind — for each other, for their child, and for the endless possibilities that awaited them.

The Martian night sky glittered with stars, a vast expanse of potential and wonder.